MEET THE GIRL TALK CHARACTERS

Sabrina Wells is petite, with curly auburn hair, sparkling hazel eyes, and a bubbly personality. Sabrina loves magazines, shopping, sleepovers, and most of all, she loves talking to her best friends.

Katie Campbell is a straight-A student and super athlete. With her blond hair, blue eyes, and matching clothes, she's everyone's idea of Lttle Miss Perfect. But Katie has a few surprises for everyone, including herself!

Randy Zak has just moved to Acorn Falls from New York City, and is she ever cool! With her radical spiked haircut and her hip New York clothes, Randy teaches everyone just how much fun it is to be different.

Allison Cloud is a Native American Indian. Allison's supersmart and really beautiful. But she has one major problem: She's thirteen years old, five foot seven, and still growing!

IT'S A SCREAM!

By L. E. Blair

GIRL TALK® series created by Western Publishing Company, Inc.

Western Publishing Company, Inc., Racine, Wisconsin 53404

Text by Susan Sloate

Chapter One

"Aaaeeeeeeeeee!"

I screamed and dived straight under one of the big cushions on our living room couch. I hid there, shivering.

"Yikes!" screamed Katie Campbell. She grabbed the cushion next to me and held on for dear life.

"Ooooh!" squealed Allison Cloud. About a millionth of a second later, she was huddled next to me with the other cushion over her face.

"Come on, guys," complained Randy Zak. "You're making such a racket I can't hear the movie!"

Randy was the only one still watching the horror video we'd rented. Katie, Allison, and I had started screaming when the movie got really gory. My name's Sabrina, by the way. And I'm *not* crazy about movies called things like *Crunching Cro-Magnon*, which is what we were

1

watching. Naturally, Randy thought it was great. She's crazy about horror movies, and somehow she'd convinced us this was a not-to-be-missed classic. We'd gone along with her, and now here we were, spending Saturday night watching a movie that three of us couldn't even look at.

"It's okay," Randy announced a few moments later. "The scene's over. You can come out now."

Cautiously I peeked over my cushion. Randy was right. Now there were just two actors talking to each other. That I could deal with.

Slowly Allison and Katie sat up, too. I couldn't believe it. Even after being scared stiff and screaming like crazy, Katie still looked neat as a pin. Her long honey-blond hair was tied back with dark purple ribbons, which looked great with the fabulous lavender oversize sweater and purple leggings she wore. Even her sneakers were purple. My favorite magazine, *Young Chic,* says you should always color-coordinate your outfits. Katie really knows how to do that.

"Randy," Katie said, laughing, "this is truly the most disgusting movie I've ever seen."

"You guys just don't like horror movies,"

Randy protested. "I've seen films that are twice as disgusting as this and not half as good."

Randy's from New York City, and she moved here to Acorn Falls, Minnesota, during the summer, right before school started. She is a very hip dresser. She has black spiked hair and the wildest clothes I've ever seen. Today she wore an oversize T-shirt, a pair of polka-dot leggings, and her favorite black granny boots. Her jewelry consisted of dangling black-and-red earrings that hung almost to her shoulders and chunky black bracelets. Black is definitely Randy's favorite color.

"Katie's right." Allison spoke up. "This is just too gory to sit through."

Allison looked a little messy. I guess one of the few disadvantages to being so tall is that it's more difficult to hide in a sofa. Although she's thirteen years old, Allison's already five seven. She looks like a model, though. Plus, she has the most amazing shiny black hair I've ever seen, maybe because she's one hundred percent Chippewa.

I'm the opposite in terms of height. I'm only four feet ten and three-quarters inches tall, so I think I have a ways to go before I stop growing.

My hair is curly and auburn, and it can get a little hard to control.

Sometimes, looking at my friends, I find it hard to believe we're so close. We all seem so different. And yet my friends are the greatest!

Finally the movie ended. As I untangled myself from the couch, my stomach started to growl. I suddenly realized that I was really hungry!

"I'm starving," I said. "Does anyone else want a snack?"

Katie grinned at me. "That was some scream, Sabs. You must have worked up a real appetite."

"I'm hungry, too," Al said. "I could eat an entire hot-fudge sundae right now."

"With lots of thick chocolate blood running down the sides," Randy added.

"Ugh! Randy!" I threw my cushion at her. "Come on, guys. Let's get some food."

Katie, Al, and I went into our kitchen, while Randy rewound the tape. I was really starving. I don't know why. Maybe watching some prehistoric guy chew up little children perks up my appetite.

"Let's have ice cream," I told my friends. "Everything on it. The works."

"*Crunching Cro-Magnon* sundaes," Al said with a laugh.

"That would be the perfect end to the evening," Katie agreed. She opened the freezer. "Anything we can't eat in here?"

"My mom said we could eat whatever we wanted to, as long as we don't touch her soup for tomorrow. So help yourself," I told her. "The sky's the limit."

Katie and Al pulled some ice cream out of the freezer, while I searched through our cupboard for special treats to put on top.

My head was all the way in the back of the cupboard when I heard a squeal from Katie. "Ugh! Oh, Sabs, this is awful! It's so *sweet!*"

I was so anxious to see what she was talking about that I banged my head inside the cupboard. For a minute I was honestly seeing stars. I shook my head to clear it, and finally Katie came into focus. "What's wrong?" I asked.

"I think your ice cream's gone bad," Katie told me. "It tastes like solid sugar."

"Can that happen?" I asked. "I thought if you kept ice cream in the freezer, it stayed good forever."

"It should stay good," Allison agreed. She

dipped her spoon cautiously into Katie's portion and tasted it. Then she made a face. "Oh," she groaned. "Katie's right. This stuff is awful!"

I couldn't understand it. Then I noticed that they were eating out of *glasses*. "Guys, that's not ice cream. That's my science project for Mr. Irving! I'm making rock candy — sugar crystals. Stop eating it — it's due in class on Tuesday!"

Katie and Allison looked a little surprised at first, but then they started to giggle. Soon we were all laughing so hard, the tears were rolling down our cheeks. Randy came into the kitchen with the videotape in her hand. "Hey, what's so funny?" she wanted to know. We couldn't tell her. We were laughing too hard. Allison was leaning against the counter, while Katie and I were doubled up on the floor.

When the phone rang, I couldn't stop laughing long enough to pick it up.

"*I'll* get it," Randy said. She grabbed the receiver. "Hello, Wells residence. This is Randy. . . . I'm a friend of Sabrina's. Who? Oh, sure. Hold on."

Randy turned to me and held out the receiver. "For you, Sabs. It's your brother, Matt."

Matt! Matt is my oldest brother, and my

favorite. He's eighteen and a freshman in college. Even though he gave me the nickname Blabs because I talk to my friends on the phone so much, I'm crazy about him.

I grabbed the phone. "Matt!" I shouted. "How are you?"

"What's going on, Blabs?" he asked. "Sounds like you're having a party."

"Just hanging out with my friends," I told him. "We just finished watching a video."

"Which one?" Matt wanted to know. He's thinking about majoring in film, so he's always interested in the movies I see and what I think of them. It makes me feel very mature when he asks my opinions. But this time I didn't think he'd be too impressed.

"It's called *Crunching Cro-Magnon*," I told him.

"Hey, that's one of my all-time favorites!" Matt said enthusiastically. "Didn't you just love it?"

"Matt! Since when are you into horror movies?" I asked. When he was still living at home, we always watched movies together, and mostly they were comedies or romances. I'd never seen him watch a horror movie!

"Come on, Sabs, this isn't your typical horror movie," Matt told me. "It's by Reginald Hatch, the greatest horror-film maker ever . . . and speaking of which, I have some incredible news for you. You're going to just flip out when I tell you." He paused dramatically.

The silence stretched out until I just couldn't stand it anymore. I was getting all excited, and I didn't even know over what! "Come on, Matt," I begged him, "at least give me a hint."

"Welllll," he said, dragging out the word, "for openers, I'm coming home for semester break."

"I know *that*," I said. I mean, I was thrilled — I never get to spend enough time with Matt — but I wasn't exactly surprised. "When will you be here?"

"On Wednesday," he told me, and I could almost hear the grin in his voice. "I'll be home for three weeks. I'm making a movie to enter in the Minnesota Film Festival."

Wow! Now I really *was* flipping out!

"Matt, that's fabulous!" I gasped. "I can't believe it! I mean, don't you have to be chosen to compete at the festival?"

"You sure do," Matt answered, and now I

could definitely hear the grin in his voice. "My film teacher loved the last short film I made, and she approved the script I just wrote for a full-length movie. She even recommended me to the review committee. *And* my all-time favorite horror-movie maker, Reginald Hatch, is going to be one of this year's judges!"

By now I was jumping up and down. I was so thrilled for Matt I couldn't even think of anything to say. Matt went on, "And, Sabs, I'm shooting the whole thing in Acorn Falls. I'll need lots of kids around your age, so spread the word at Bradley, will you? I'll start auditioning first thing next Saturday morning."

"Oh, Matt!" Now I was sure I was going to flip out. "Does that mean I could . . ."

"You could very possibly." Matt laughed. He knew all about my big dream of becoming an actress. "But listen, Sabs, no favoritism. If you're really good, you'll get a part. If not . . ."

"That's okay, Matt, I understand," I assured him. Besides, I'd been working very hard on my acting all year, and I'd already been in school productions of *Grease* and *The Wizard of Oz*. If that isn't solid experience, I don't know what is.

Matt was still talking, but I was so excited I

could hardly listen. He was coming home for semester break, and he'd be making a movie to enter in the Minnesota Film Festival — and I might even be able to get a part in the movie! How much more excitement could anybody stand in one night?

When I hung up, my friends crowded around me. They could tell that something really big had just happened and wanted the details.

"Come on, Sabs," Randy demanded, "tell us what's happened."

"You look like you're about ready to burst open," Katie observed. "It must be something out of this world."

"Is it ever!" I sputtered. "Hang on to your hats, guys — the absolutely most thrilling thing you can imagine is about to happen right here in Acorn Falls!"

Chapter Two

On Wednesday I was still so excited that I could hardly pay attention to what I was doing in class. In fact, by last period, when I have science, I had no idea what gloppy mess I was staring at through the microscope.

"Sabrina!" called Mr. Irving, our substitute science teacher. I looked up. All the other kids were looking into their microscopes and writing furiously in their notebooks. Mr. Irving was staring at me. "Why aren't you working?" he asked.

"Well, I . . ." I didn't want to tell him that I was too excited to work.

Mr. Irving was substituting for our regular teacher, Miss Miller, who would be away a few weeks taking care of a sick relative. Mr. Irving was tall and thin and weird-looking. He was always squinting. I was never really sure whether he was blind as a bat or just a little strange.

I'd heard rumors that Mr. Irving was some kind of genius and that Mr. Hansen, the principal, had agreed to let him use the school's labs after class time for his own experiments. For all I knew, he was inventing a cure for cancer. But he also seemed a little creepy. There was something not exactly right about him. But who knows? Maybe all geniuses are like that.

"Sabrina!" Mr. Irving was beginning to sound a little annoyed. "I asked why you weren't working."

"I'm sorry, Mr. Irving." I gulped, fumbling for an explanation. "I . . . I guess my mind's not really on the work today."

"Oh? You have a more serious problem?" Mr. Irving asked. Somehow I didn't think now was the time to discuss my acting ambitions.

"Oh, no, thank you. I'll get right to work." I opened my notebook to a blank page and glanced up at everybody else. They were finishing up and putting their microscopes away.

Mr. Irving called Winslow Barton to collect the microscopes, which meant I didn't get a thing written down. Then Mr. Irving collected all the papers. When he saw my blank paper, he just shook his head.

"You are going to have to finish this assignment after school today, Sabrina," said Mr. Irving.

After school! But Matt was coming home tonight, and I wanted to help my mother get ready. But I also knew that my science grades were nothing to write home about. Science is my least favorite subject, next to math, and there was no way I could afford to mess up an assignment.

"Okay, I'll start right on it," I said quickly.

"Well," Mr. Irving said, glancing at the big clock hanging over the door, "if you read the experiment and answer the last set of questions, I'll consider the assignment finished. However, I have an appointment this afternoon and I don't want to be late for it."

"I'll hurry," I promised.

"You must promise to get the assignment done and not daydream," he added.

"Absolutely. Thanks, Mr. Irving," I said. "I'll just get my stuff and come right back."

When the bell rang, I started filing out with the others. Then somebody shouted, "Hey! Look out there! Fog again!"

I couldn't help stopping to look out the big

windows in the lab. A huge cloud of fog was rolling in, moving so fast it looked like it was going to cover the school in a minute. I hate fog, and we'd had a lot of foggy days recently. It was getting to be downright spooky just walking home from school.

Then I noticed that Mr. Irving was looking at me. Uh-oh, I had promised to be quick. I hurried out of the room and tried to get to my locker and back quickly, but the halls were crowded. Everybody was rushing to get home.

By the time I got back to Mr. Irving's room, he was glancing impatiently at the clock. "Well, Sabrina," he said, "I wasn't sure you were going to make it."

"I'm sorry, Mr. Irving," I said, sliding quickly into my seat. "I just stopped to look at the fog. We've had so much fog in Acorn Falls the last week or so."

Mr. Irving handed me a microscope, a slide, and a sheet of questions. "That's perfectly natural, Sabrina. When we get a spell of warm weather in the wintertime, fog usually occurs."

"I see," I said, opening my notebook as fast as I could. Mr. Irving was glancing at the clock again, so I didn't want to waste his time. "I just couldn't help thinking it would be a great night for monsters and zombies and other creepy things."

Oh, great! Where did that come from? It must have been those dumb horror movies Randy keeps talking about. Why did I have to say that in front of Mr. Irving? Now he'd really think I was a bingo head.

Mr. Irving looked at me sharply as I placed the slide under the microscope and started to adjust the lens. "Why do you say that, Sabrina?"

He was looking at me in the strangest way. "It just looks really spooky outside, that's all," I said.

I got down to work, looking into the eyepiece of the microscope. In a minute, though, Mr. Irving looked up at the clock and said abruptly, "Well, I have some things to collect. You'll be all right here, won't you? I'll be back in a few minutes."

"Oh, yes, Mr. Irving, I'll be fine," I assured him.

"Excellent," he said. Then he bolted from the room. I couldn't believe it! He was acting like a kid who was late for school. I decided to try and get the experiment done quickly. Then I could get home, too. I couldn't wait to see Matt.

It only took me about ten minutes to write down answers to all the questions on Mr. Irving's sheet. But when I looked up, Mr. Irving still hadn't come back.

I waited, thinking that I shouldn't leave until he gave me permission. But time was going by, and I was getting more and more impatient to be home. Finally, when fifteen minutes had passed and there was still no sign of Mr. Irving, I put the microscope, the slide, and my paper on Mr. Irving's big lab table.

There was a window open, and a breeze was blowing into the room. I didn't want my paper to blow away, so I put the microscope on top of it as a paperweight.

Then I noticed that the door behind Mr. Irving's desk, which led to a little storage area, was slightly ajar. I just couldn't help myself. I peeked in.

Inside was the neatest miniature laboratory I'd ever seen! There were all kinds of interesting mixtures in test tubes, with rubber tubing connecting everything together. I couldn't believe it! This had to be Mr. Irving's private work. I wondered what kind of experiments he was doing.

I looked closer at the tubes. They were all full of a deep ruby-red liquid, with some orange in the bottom. If I hadn't known better, I would have sworn it looked like blood!

Suddenly I thought I heard someone come into the classroom behind me. I quickly left the little room and looked around. No one was there.

I picked up my backpack and jacket and hurried out the side door of school. I could see the traffic light at the bottom of the hill was about to change and I started to run. Maybe I could just make it.

I was too late. Just as I got to the corner, the light turned red and cars started flowing past. I pressed the button that changed the sign from DON'T WALK to WALK and waited.

The sign was taking forever to change. After a while it seemed as though there weren't any cars coming at all. I was more impatient than ever, so after looking both ways, I stepped off the curb.

Screech! A white car that looked like it was left over from the sixties was chugging right at me, and had managed to stop just an inch or so away from my legs! Startled and terrified, I turned to look at the driver. It was Mr. Irving!

"Mr. Irving!" I gasped. "You almost hit me!"

Mr. Irving was already hurrying toward me. "Sabrina! Are you all right?"

"I-I think so," I said, trying to stop trembling.

"Now, it's all right," Mr. Irving said as he looked me over carefully. "I don't think there's a single scratch."

"Mr. Irving, didn't you even see me on the curb?" I asked.

"I must have been daydreaming," he admitted. "I'm terribly sorry, Sabrina."

By now I had caught my breath and was no longer trembling. It was true that his car hadn't touched me, but just the same, it could have been a really nasty accident.

I opened my mouth to say something, but Mr. Irving was already getting back into his car. "Well, see you in class tomorrow," he said. He started up the car and chugged off.

I watched the car drive away. Then I saw something that really shocked me. The trunk of Mr. Irving's car didn't seem to be shut properly. It was tied closed with some twine that didn't quite do the job, so the trunk was slightly open. There was something sticking out of it. I could swear it was a human hand!

"Ohmygosh!" I gasped. I tried to take deep breaths and calm down, but my heart was pounding a mile a minute. Maybe it wasn't a hand, I reasoned with myself. Maybe I was just seeing things. But my eyesight is twenty-twenty, and I knew for sure that whatever was attached to that hand was something I didn't even want to think about.

First the fog, then that red stuff in Mr. Irving's lab, and now this hand? I hurried across the street. I figured I'd better get home and start making sense of what I'd seen!

Chapter Three

On the way home all I could think about was Mr. Irving, his lab, and the hand I'd seen. There was something strange going on, and I was determined to get to the bottom of it. But when I turned the corner onto my street, I started feeling excited about seeing my brother Matt. Matt hadn't been home since Christmas vacation three months ago, and I couldn't wait to see him.

I burst into the house and immediately ran into four huge suitcases sitting right in the middle of the hall. "Ooops!" I said as I tumbled over the luggage.

"Look out, Sabs!" came Matt's voice from the upstairs hall.

It was too late for that now. My backpack had fallen to the floor, and my legs were tangled up with those giant suitcases. I could hardly move!

The next thing I knew, Matt was downstairs, hugging me and untangling me from the suitcases. He pulled me up and patted my hair. "Hi, babe," he said. Matt thinks it's very cool and "cinema" to call everyone "babe."

"Oh, Matt!" I said, hugging him. He's lots taller than me, of course. In fact, he's over six feet tall. He has nice dark brown hair and hazel eyes, which always seem to twinkle when he smiles. They were twinkling now. It was fantastic to see him.

"I'm so glad you're home," I told him. "I can't wait to hear all about your movie."

"I've got the script with me," Matt said with a grin. "Want to read it tonight?"

"That would be awesome!" I practically yelled. "Are you really going to use Bradley kids? Am I really going to be in it? What's it about?"

"Calm down, Sabs." Matt laughed. "You'll get your shot at stardom. Listen, can you still do that great scream?"

"Scream? What do I need to scream for?" I asked. Suddenly I had this terrible feeling I wouldn't want to hear the answer.

Sure enough, Matt answered, "I'm going to make a real old-fashioned horror movie. Just like Reginald Hatch does. Lots of blood and gore . . .

and *lots* of screaming."

I should have known. Matt was obviously really into horror movies these days. I mean, he'd known all about *Crunching Cro-Magnon* and Reginald Hatch. Oh, well, maybe there was something I could do. Maybe I could be a victim or an extra. He would need lots of those. Maybe . . .

"Hey, Matt, are you going to introduce me?" came a voice from above.

I looked up and saw the absolutely most amazing guy I'd ever seen in my whole life! He was tall and had golden hair and huge dark eyes. For a minute I thought maybe I was hallucinating. Maybe that near accident with Mr. Irving had jarred something loose in my brain after all. Who *was* this incredible guy?

"Sabs, meet my roommate, Brent Rogers," Matt announced as Brent came down the stairs. "Brent, this is my little sister, Sabrina."

I gave Brent the biggest smile I could and at the same time kicked Matt in the ankle. "You didn't have to call me 'little,'" I whispered at him.

"Brent's going to star in the movie," Matt explained, rubbing his ankle and glaring at me.

"He's playing the mad scientist."

Brent a mad scientist? Either he was one amazing actor, or this was going to be a very unusual horror picture. Brent didn't look like a mad scientist. He looked like a very young Robert Redford. Only more so. I decided to re-think my attitude toward horror movies. I already knew that I really wanted to be in this one.

Brent gave me a warm, friendly smile and shook my hand. "Glad to meet you, Sabrina," he said. "Matt tells me you're a terrific actress."

"Thanks," I replied as I started blushing. I realized that if Brent and I were both in the movie, we'd be seeing a lot of each other. That would be awesome!

That night at dinner I couldn't believe the difference it made having two more at the table. Usually it's pretty noisy and crowded with Luke, Mark, and Sam — my other brothers — plus me and my parents. Now, with Matt and Brent at the table as well, it was pandemonium! Everybody was squeezed together so tightly, we could hard-ly breathe; and we all talked so much, nobody could hear a thing.

The good news was, Brent was seated right

next to me. And since there was so little room —
and since he was a lefty — we kept bumping
elbows all through dinner. Every time that happened, Brent smiled at me and I got this warm,
squishy feeling in my stomach.

When it had quieted down a little, my dad
asked Matt about the movie. Matt explained that
he planned to film it in our backyard and on the
school grounds at Bradley. He'd written to Mr.
Hansen asking for permission, and Mr. Hansen
had replied that it would be fine. He thought
that having a film made at Bradley would be
good publicity for the school, even if it was a
horror movie.

"And you said you'd be using Bradley students as actors?" my dad asked. He gave me a
quick look. I guess he knew how much I wanted
to be in Matt's movie.

"Right," Matt replied. "Sabs, Sam, and Mark
are already spreading the word about auditions.
I thought we could have them Saturday in the
garage."

"That sounds like a great idea, Matt," my
mom said, clearing the plates away.

"There's just one problem I haven't solved
yet," Matt said quietly.

But speaking of problems reminded me of mine with Mr. Irving. "You won't believe what happened to me today!" I blurted out.

Everyone was still really interested in talking to Matt, but they could tell I had something important to say.

"Okay, Sabrina," my dad said. "What happened?"

"I almost got run over by my substitute science teacher, Mr. Irving!" I told them all about his weird laboratory and the dark red stuff in the test tubes and how I saw a hand sticking out of the trunk of his car when he drove away.

There was a little silence when I finished. Finally Luke spoke. "This time, Sabs, I think you have definitely flipped your wig."

"Yeah, Sabs," Sam chimed in. Sam's my twin brother, and he's older than me by four whole minutes, which he seems to think is a big deal. "In a minute you'll be telling us Mr. Irving spends his evenings digging up bodies to experiment on."

"Stop it, you guys!" I said angrily. "I'm not making this up! It really happened! And no matter what you say, I think Mr. Irving is definitely weird!"

"Irving . . ." Matt said. "Is he new?"

"Yes," I said, "he's a sub. He just moved here from Minneapolis."

Brent looked at Matt. Matt looked at Brent. "See, I told you he moved here," Matt said. He looked really interested. "Do you know this Irving's first name?" he asked me.

"Well, I saw him sign a requisition form once," I said. "He just wrote 'T. Irving' in this big slanty handwriting."

Matt and Brent gave each other a high-five. "Tennessee Irving," they said together.

"It's gotta be," Matt said. He grinned with relief. "Maybe this solves my little problem after all!"

Everybody started talking at once after that, so I couldn't find out how Mr. Irving could help Matt. It got really noisy. My mom finally held up her hand for silence. "When will you start actually shooting?"

"We figured we'd be ready to go by next Tuesday or Wednesday," Brent answered. "And, Mrs. Wells, I can't thank you enough for letting me stay here at the house during the shoot."

Wow! Brent, that gorgeous hunk, was going to be staying here in our house for the whole time they were making the movie! I couldn't stand it. It was just too thrilling to think about. That meant we'd see each other every single day! I couldn't wait to tell my friends. A mad scientist and a gorgeous college student playing a mad scientist all in one day!

Chapter Four

On Friday night my friends and I had a sleep-over at Katie's house. Katie's mom recently married a very nice man who moved them into a huge mansion. It is so big that we can make lots of noise and usually not disturb anyone.

You see, the auditions for Matt's movie were on Saturday morning and we wanted to practice for them. We were all trying out, even Katie and Allison, who aren't really into acting. The idea of being in a movie was just so exciting, no one could resist.

I'd read the script for Matt's movie over the past few days and told my friends all about it. The movie was about a new kid in a small town. He can't make friends with anyone because they think he's weird. So the kid, who's really a brilliant mad scientist, figures out a way to control the kids' minds and slowly turns them all into zombies. Then the kids, who are being controlled by the mad scientist, attack all the adults in town. It gets very bloody and gory at the end. Eventually the mad scientist gets killed by a posse of students who've resisted the mind control.

We all had special little bits we needed to rehearse. Katie wanted to practice running while looking over her shoulder, Allison was learning to do an awesome faint, Randy was really getting into zombie walking, and I wanted to work on my scream. We had even managed to work it all into a scene. It was awesome! Randy would start walking after Katie with her arms stuck straight out in front of her. Katie would run away from her. Then I'd see them and scream really loudly, which would make Allison faint.

***

"Okay," Katie said early Saturday morning. "Here we go." We'd decided to try our scene once more before getting ready to leave for my house.

From somewhere behind me I heard Katie come running toward me. Then she zoomed by. I turned around and saw Randy coming at me. "Aaaeeeeeeeee!" I screamed at the top of my lungs. Allison, who had been standing next to me, crumpled onto the floor.

Then I saw Emily, Katie's older sister, standing in the door of the living room, where we'd been rehearsing. She was wearing a bathrobe and didn't look too happy. "Kids," she said, shaking her head. "You never know what they'll be up to next. Would you guys mind *not* screaming or running around before ten o'clock. Some of us need to sleep."

Katie looked really apologetic. "I'm sorry, Emily," she said. "I guess we got a little carried away."

"Yeah," I said. "I'm sorry, too. We'll stop now, I promise."

Emily went back to bed, and we tiptoed into the kitchen to get some breakfast.

"Well, I'm sorry we disturbed your sister," said Randy. "But that last run was awesome."

"Yeah," said Allison. "I think we are all ready for the auditions."

"That last scream was the best one you've ever done, Sabs," said Katie. "You really sounded scared."

"I think you've got it," Allison agreed. "I can't imagine anybody screaming better than that."

Randy frowned. "Doesn't yelling like that hurt your throat? I mean, what happens if you have to do it ten or twelve times in a row?"

"No problem," I said confidently. "It doesn't hurt at all. I feel great."

Someone had left the newspaper on the kitchen table. I opened it to the horoscope column. I try to read my horoscope every morning. It helps me get through the day when I know what to expect. I read everybody's horoscope out loud. Mine said, "A day of tension and possible upset. Stay calm no matter what. All will turn out the way you want."

"For once, that sounds like good advice," Randy said. "Just keep cool no matter what, Sabs. That's the only way to get through this audition."

Actually, I'd been trying to stay cool the past two days in school, although it hadn't been easy. I'd told everyone about the auditions for Matt's movie. A lot of people were thrilled at the idea of appearing in a movie, and I was pretty sure most of them would show up for the auditions.

On Friday, in fact, I was sitting in the cafeteria with my friends when Allison said quietly, "Don't look now, but here comes Cameron

Booth."

I couldn't believe it! Cameron had played Danny in *Grease* and he was one of the dreamiest guys in school. The only class we were in together was band, but whenever I saw him, he was always supernice.

Cameron walked right up to the table and asked me what time the boys should be at my house to audition for the film. "Matt said he would be looking at the boys in the afternoon," I told him, my heart hammering. He looked totally amazing in his dark sweater and blue shirt. "So if you want to come by around one o'clock, that should be fine."

"Thanks, Sabrina," Cameron replied, smiling warmly at me. "I hope we'll get a chance to work together again."

"Me too," I said. Cameron smiled at me again and then went to sit with a group of his friends. I couldn't stop thinking about how awesome it would be to be in a movie with both Brent *and* Cameron!

I shook my head to clear it and bring myself back to Saturday morning. By now it was nine-thirty, time to get ready for the auditions, which started at eleven.

One of the reasons we'd had the sleepover at Katie's was that she had enough bathrooms to go around, so we could all get ready at the same time. Surviving in my house was difficult these days. Just having two extra boys in the house had made it impossible to have enough bathroom time. I had to get up really early in the morning just to get into the shower, and as soon as I turned the water off, someone was banging on the door, demanding that I hurry up. There was certainly no time to do anything special with my hair or anything. And for the auditions I wanted to look good. So we decided to stay at Katie's and all get ready together.

I'd even decided what I was going to wear beforehand so I could bring it with me. I figured that a girl in a horror movie should look fragile and frightened — so I picked out my favorite overalls and a soft, thin, lacy long-sleeved green sweater underneath. That way, I thought I'd look even smaller and more helpless when the zombies showed up.

I took a long, luxurious shower in Katie's bathroom and washed my hair thoroughly. After I blew my hair dry, I braided the top section and fastened it with a small bow. Then I brushed the rest loose so it hung in curls on my shoulders. When I'd finished my hair, I wriggled into my outfit. I left one strap of the overalls unbuckled.

"You look great," Katie said approvingly.

"Yeah," said Randy. "You look like a school-girl."

I giggled. "That's the idea. Besides, if you want to get technical about it, I *am* a schoolgirl. You guys all look awesome, too," I said.

They all looked great! Randy was the most outrageous, as usual. She was wearing this really cool black-and-white-checkered top that had a big black swirl on the back. If you looked at the swirl for too long, you could get dizzy. Randy really wanted to play a zombie in the movie.

Katie and Allison looked more normal. They wanted to play students at the school, so they tried to look as average as possible. Allison was wearing jeans with a series of holes cut in them in a pattern. She had an oversize red sweater, plus a red bandanna in her hair. Katie look awesome in her fuchsia cardigan and pink leggings. Her headband matched the sweater exactly. If Matt was picking actors by how great they looked, my friends would be in for sure.

I looked back into the mirror to put some

final touches on my hair. I didn't look quite right. Something was definitely missing.

Oh, no! The makeup! I've got a tiny bottle of light foundation, which I'm only allowed to wear for very special occasions and when I'm onstage, to lighten my freckles. I suddenly remembered that I'd left it on a shelf in the bathroom at my house. Since someone was in there when I was packing, I'd forgotten all about it.

"What am I going to do about my freckles?" I wailed. "I wanted to use my foundation on them, but I left it at home! And I'll never get back in that bathroom before the auditions!"

Katie looked carefully at my freckles. "Honestly, Sabs, they're hardly even noticeable. Besides, Matt knows you have freckles. What difference will it make if he sees them or not?"

"It'll ruin my whole look," I insisted. "I've got to use something to get rid of them."

Katie thought hard. "I can't borrow any makeup from Emily," she said. "Not after we disturbed her."

"Maybe you don't have to use actual makeup," Allison suggested. "How about using something else?"

"Like what?" I asked.

We all peered into her open medicine cabinet. Suddenly my eye caught a tin of baby powder. "How about powder?"

"Baby powder? On freckles?" Randy said skeptically.

I took the powder down off the shelf and hunted for a powder puff, but I couldn't find one. "I guess you'll just have to pour it on and hope for the best," Randy said.

I was ready to pour out the powder when Allison noticed the time. "You know, guys," she said, "it's already ten forty-five. If we don't leave right now, we're going to be late."

"No problem," Randy said. "We'll make it."

I put the powder into my duffel bag. "Mom said she'd pick us up about now," I said. "We've still got fifteen minutes. Come on."

Chapter Five

Twelve minutes later we got to my house. Matt and Brent were already arranging chairs and tables. My friends and I started helping Matt set up.

"This is so cool," Randy called to me as she and Allison each lugged in a couple of chairs and put them in a neat row. "I loved helping my dad with his videos in New York. Looks like I'll be able to do some crew work for your brother, too."

I was really psyched. Randy's father was a director of music videos and commercials in New York, and Randy always glowed when she talked about his work. I knew she'd be a great help to Matt on the movie.

Right at eleven, Matt looked out at the street. Kids were hanging out on our lawn and far down the block.

"Good morning, everybody!" Matt called out

to the kids through this big megaphone. "Welcome to the auditions for *Last Scream of the Zombies*. I promise you we'll be seeing everybody, so you'll all get a chance to show us what you can do. Right now, though, we'll be starting with the girls.

"I'll need two actresses to play the heroine and her best friend, and then a number of other actresses to play victims, who'll either die or turn into zombies," Matt went on. "So, one at a time, I'd like you to come up to this table, give us your name and previous acting experience, and read from the script."

In about two seconds flat, the girls had formed a line straight down the block. When I looked at it, I couldn't even see the end. Every girl from Bradley Junior High must have come!

I was still so excited that I didn't even realize I had to stand in line. "Sabs," Matt said quietly, "you'd better get in line, too."

I just looked at him. He couldn't mean going all the way to the end, could he? That could be blocks from here! I might be standing in line for hours before I could audition — and after all, I was his sister!

"Sabs," Matt said again. "I'd like to start."

"Oh, Matt . . ." I said. But there wasn't anything Matt could do. I knew he wanted to be impartial and handle things properly. The only way to be fair was for me to stand in line.

Slowly I walked past the line of waiting girls, my head down. Suddenly I heard a voice. "Sabs! Over here!"

I turned and saw Katie waving at me. She, Randy, and Allison were standing in line, holding a place for me. Best of all, there were only about fifteen or so girls ahead of them! What a break!

I hurried over to them. "I figured we'd better get in line or we'd have to wait forever," Randy said.

"Thanks a million," I said, giving them all hugs. "Now I can fix my freckles and listen to the other readings at the same time."

"Good idea," Katie agreed. I reached into my duffel bag for a mirror, and she held it up so I could examine my face. I noticed right away that my face was all red from the rushing around we'd done to get to the auditions on time. I'd need a lot of powder to cover up not only my freckles but the bright red in my cheeks!

Just then I heard a voice ahead of me. "Well,

look at that: Sabrina's trying to change the way she looks just before she reads for the movie. But I don't think we have that kind of time."

Oh, no! I knew Stacy Hansen's voice when I heard it! Even though Stacy's in the seventh grade, too, she thinks she's far cooler than the rest of us. She acts so stuck up, my friends and I call her Stacy the Great. Sure enough, Stacy was in line, too, several places in front of us. I guess I didn't see her when I got in line with my friends.

Eva Malone and Laurel Spencer, two of Stacy's clones, were with her. Stacy was wearing this shiny blue jumpsuit with a fluffy blue scarf at her throat. I began to feel a little shabby in my overalls.

"Don't let her get to you," Katie whispered. "She's just trying to get you rattled so you won't read well. Take it easy."

Right. I vowed that I'd remember my horoscope and relax. Everything good was supposed to be coming my way today. All I had to do was sit back and wait for it to happen.

As Matt greeted the first girl in line, I got to work with the baby powder. Since I didn't have a powder puff, I just spilled the powder into my hand and patted it on my face.

"She looks like a clown in the circus!" Eva shrieked. She was looking right at me, so it was obvious who she was talking about.

I took a quick look at myself in the mirror Katie was holding. I did look a little too pale, with all that white slathered over my face. But at least my freckles were pretty much covered up. I just couldn't help thinking I looked a little like one of those marble statues that came to life.

If I wipe some off, it'll be fine, I told myself. I fumbled in the duffel bag for a tissue and dusted off my face as fast as I could. Matt and Brent were already finished with the first two girls, and I could see that Stacy would be next. I really wanted to listen to her audition.

Stacy walked haughtily up to the table where Matt and Brent sat. "I'm Stacy Hansen," she informed them. "My father's the principal of Bradley."

"Nice to meet you, Stacy," said Brent with a warm smile. I hoped that didn't mean he already liked Stacy. Maybe he's just trying to put her at ease, I decided. That was awfully nice of him.

"Tell us about your acting experience," Matt suggested.

"Well, I've had quite a lot," Stacy said,

sounding very sure of herself. "I've been taking singing, dancing, and piano lessons since I was four, and recently I played Sandy in the Bradley production of *Grease* and Dorothy in *The Wizard of Oz.*"

"Very impressive," Brent said. He held out a script to her. "How about reading this scene with me?"

"Oh, I'd love to," Stacy gushed. Katie and I exchanged a look. When Stacy wants to be sweet, nobody does it better. She read over the scene to herself, then said to Brent, "I'm all ready."

"Fine," Brent said. "Let's go."

He started the scene, and Stacy responded. It took place between the mad scientist and his best friend, Andrea, the girl who really believes he's good. I'd loved the part when I read it and was dying to play it myself. Now, though, watching Stacy, I wasn't sure I'd ever get the chance.

"Thank you, Stacy," Matt said when she'd finished. He looked very impressed. "That was very good. Now, one more thing. Would you mind screaming for us?"

"Screaming?" Stacy looked a little unsure of

herself. "You mean a real scream?"

"Like you just saw a ghost," Matt told her. "The scariest scream you can do."

"Okay," said Stacy. She took a deep breath, then shrieked as loud as she could.

It was the worst sound I'd ever heard come out of a human throat! Stacy sounded like a fire whistle or car alarm! I could see the kids in line near the front holding their ears. Even Brent and Matt seemed to wince a little.

"Thank you," Matt said. "That's just fine. Now if I can have your phone number . . ." Stacy gave it to him, sounding a little smug. Obviously she thought she'd done just great. "We'll be in touch in a few days," Matt added.

"No hurry," Stacy said sweetly. "Take your time." She walked off with this sultry starlet walk.

"Relax, Sabs," Katie whispered to me. "You scream a thousand times better than that. Wait'll they hear it."

I was a lot more worried about how my face looked with all that powder on it. I concentrated frantically on wiping off as much as I could without my freckles showing up again. It seemed like the following auditions went like lightning.

"Next," Matt called.

I was next. Nervously I walked up to the table. "Hi," I said. "You don't really need my name and phone number, do you?"

Brent grinned. "If we can't find you, we haven't got any business trying to make a movie," he said. "You know about her acting experience, Matt?"

"In excruciating detail." Matt laughed. "She writes me long letters at school, giving me the reviews and everything."

I could feel my body blush coming on. That's when my whole body turns red from the top of my scalp to the bottom of my feet. It's impossible to hide, and I always just want to die of embarrassment.

Brent was already handing me the script and explaining the part of Andrea. He told me to read it over and get ready, and then we'd read through it together. Brent was wonderful to work with. He gave me lots of time to react to his lines and didn't try to rush me or anything. I felt a thousand times better when we'd finished. Even if he was my brother, Matt would have to admit I was becoming a good actress.

"Thank you, Sabrina," Matt said very formally when I'd finished. "That'll be all. We'll be in touch in a few days."

"Just a minute," Randy spoke up. "Don't you want to hear her scream?"

Brent and Matt exchanged a look. "I don't think that's necessary," Matt said finally.

"Oh, please," I begged. I knew my scream was better than Stacy's. "I want the same chance as every other girl here."

Matt glared at me. He knew just what my scream sounded like, but he couldn't exactly refuse to let me audition the same way the others did. "All right, Sabrina," he said finally. "Let 'er rip."

I took a deep breath. I could see Stacy standing by the curb, watching me. I let go. It was definitely the best scream I'd ever done. You could hear it all the way down the street! Katie, Randy, and Allison cheered. Even the boys waiting at the curb seemed impressed. I caught the look on Cameron Booth's face. He looked stunned.

My horoscope was right. All I had to do was stay calm, and it would turn out the way I wanted.

Chapter Six

It was foggy again that night, but I was too excited about the auditions to care. Matt and Brent had spent all day hearing kids read for the parts. After that, they closed the door to Matt's room and talked over the actors. Any minute now, Matt would be coming downstairs with the cast list.

Randy called just before dinner. "Want to rent a movie tonight, Sabs?" she asked. "It's a perfect night for something really spooky. You could even practice your screams while we watch!" She laughed.

"No, thanks!" I retorted, laughing also. "I've done enough screaming for one day! Besides, Matt's almost finished with the cast list. I want to be here to find out who'll be in it. Why don't you guys come over here?"

"Sure," said Randy. "But you know you're in. After that scream, I think most of the neighborhood dogs still have earaches. And did you see the look on Stacy's face? She knew it was all over, too. Don't worry."

I wanted to believe Randy, but I wanted the part so badly that I was afraid to think positive thoughts. I was too scared of being let down if Matt picked someone else for the part of Andrea. And what if he didn't put me in the movie at all?

I'll just think about something else, I told myself as I set the table for dinner.

"I can't believe it," my mom said. She was making out a shopping list. "It seems like we've been running out of food ever since Matt and Brent came home. I'll have to start buying twice as much!" She peered into the cupboards. "We've used up an awful lot of staples. Look at that: no flour, no sugar. . . . And this is really odd: they've even been into the red vegetable dye. There's only a tiny bit left."

"Sorry, Mrs. Wells," Brent apologized, coming into the kitchen. "We were experimenting with blood. We tried flour and sugar and red vegetable dye, but it turned out pretty gloppy."

"I can imagine." My mom laughed. "Looks like you'll have to keep experimenting."

"I guess so," Matt agreed. He was right

behind Brent. "We could just use regular fake blood, but I don't think it will look right on the kind of film I'm using. And I really want it to look real."

Then I noticed that Matt was holding a type-written list. I couldn't take my eyes off it.

Matt saw me staring. "Okay, Sabs, you've caught me." He grinned. "We've made the final decisions. This is the cast list."

"Oh, Matt," I breathed. I couldn't beg him to put me in the movie. I was too mature and pro-fessional for that. But I wanted to be in this movie more than anything in the world. Besides, if Matt didn't think enough of me to cast me and he was my own brother, I was in real trouble. I could see my whole career hinging on this movie. I just *had* to get a part!

"Shall we tell her, Brent?" Matt asked with a very straight face.

My mom saw the pleading look in my eyes. "Now, Matt, don't tease your sister. Just tell her and get it over with."

"Okay," Matt said. He gave me a solemn look. "The truth is, Sabs, we just couldn't find anyone in Acorn Falls who screams like you do. You'll be playing Andrea in the movie."

Andrea! That was the part I wanted! I threw my arms around Matt. "Oh, thank you, thank you!" I shouted. "I can't believe it!"

Sam walked in while I was dancing around the dining room. He looked at me in mock disgust. "There she goes again," he said. "She gets one part in a movie and becomes totally unglued."

Brent gave him a grin. "Oh, then I guess it's not important to you. Your part in the movie, I mean."

"*My* part!" Sam yelled. "What part did I get?"

"You'll be playing Ned," Matt informed him. "He's the leader of the kids who get together a posse to stop the mad scientist."

"Hey, Sabs!" Sam shouted. "I'm going to be a star, too!" We both danced around the dining room. Matt and Brent stood there laughing at us, so we dragged them into our dance. I think my mom thought we'd finally lost it.

By Monday afternoon everyone at Bradley knew who was in the movie. Almost all of the seventh graders got chosen for extras, including Allison and Katie. But they decided they'd rather just help out around the set than be on-screen. Randy got a small role as a friend of Andrea's who gets turned into a zombie by the mad scientist. She was really excited. Sam's friends Nick Robbins and Jason McKee were playing students who help Sam's character form the posse. Cameron was playing the brainy science student who tries to figure out a scientific way of changing the zombies back into humans.

Stacy bragged all over school about her part. She was playing the mad scientist's first victim, a lovely young student who innocently wanders into his laboratory and frightens him while he's at work. Naturally, he has to turn her into a zombie.

"It's a very important part," Stacy was saying in the cafeteria during lunch. "Matt can only trust it to someone who has real talent."

Oh, please. I pretended not to hear Stacy but concentrated instead on my salad. I'd decided to be extracareful in my self-improvement program during the making of the film. Everybody knows that the camera adds ten pounds to your weight automatically. So you have to be even thinner than normal to look right. I was sticking to salads and lean meats like chicken and fish until the last day of shooting was over.

"Can you believe Stacy?" Randy said, chewing on her apple. "You don't hear Sabs going around bragging about her part. And she's got the biggest role in the film, next to Brent."

"Sabs would never go around bragging about herself," Katie said loyally. She spooned up some yogurt and pointed it at Stacy. "In fact, she'd never be caught dead acting so puffed up."

It gave me a nice, warm feeling to know that my friends thought I was down to earth, not stuck up like Stacy. After all, I told myself, the important thing is to do a good job as an actress. The rest doesn't matter.

"Anyway," Randy said, "we still have to go to class every day, even if we are making a movie."

"That's true," Allison agreed. "Our teachers aren't going to stop giving assignments just because of Matt's movie."

"Speaking of which," Katie said to me, "are you and Randy doing a unit about electricity in Mr. Irving's class? That's what we're doing in my class."

Randy and I looked at each other. "I don't think so," I said, shaking my head. "In fact, Mr. Irving told us that today we're going to be starting something totally new. He didn't say what."

"He's kind of strange," Randy added, "but I think he's okay."

"I don't know," said Katie. "Almost running Sabs over . . . that doesn't sound too nice to me."

I had told my friends about my strange after-school experience with Mr. Irving.

"Well, let's not jump to conclusions," Allison put in. Al's always careful to give people the benefit of the doubt. That's part of what makes her such a good friend. "Maybe he's just a little eccentric. If he's as smart as everyone says, maybe he just spends more time thinking than watching where he's going. I'm sure he didn't mean to hurt you, Sabrina."

"I don't think so, either," I assured her. "But still, why was there a hand sticking out of the trunk of his car?"

"Maybe he hit somebody else on his way over," Randy said with a giggle. We all burst out laughing. Just then the bell rang, and there was no more time to speculate about Mr. Irving.

That afternoon, when Randy and I got to Mr. Irving's room, we looked around in surprise. Usually he had our microscopes and test tubes already set out on his big lab table. Sometimes he'd even passed out lists of questions by the time we arrived. Today, though, there were no microscopes and no test tubes. Mr. Irving wasn't even wearing his usual white lab coat. He just leaned against his desk, waiting for us to get seated. Behind him, written on the blackboard, was one single word: "Hypnosis."

We all sat down and got quiet. Then Mr. Irving held up his hand. "How many of you have ever been hypnotized?" he asked.

Wow! That was something I sure didn't expect. I looked around the room. To my amazement, Randy raised her hand. She was the only one. Mr. Irving called on her.

"All right, Randy," he said. "Suppose you tell us what you know about hypnosis."

"Well, it's a state of deep relaxation," Randy answered.

"That's right," Mr. Irving said. "Deep relaxation. The place where you are receptive to suggestion." He looked around. "Why would someone want to be hypnotized?"

Winslow Barton raised his hand. That made sense. Winslow was a brain. He seemed to know something about everything. Mr. Irving called on him. "Hypnosis is a little like mind control. It can be a way of dealing with bad habits," Winslow said. "If you want to stop smoking or have a good night's sleep, hypnosis can help you achieve those things while you're susceptible to posthypnotic suggestion."

"What does that mean: 'susceptible to post-hypnotic suggestion'?" Mr. Irving asked.

I raised my hand. Mr. Irving called on me. "If you want to stop doing something, a hypnotist can tell you not to do that thing in the future," I said. It sounded a little vague, but Mr. Irving seemed to understand. He nodded for me to go on. "Like, if you want to stop smoking, the hypnotist will put you under, then tell you while you're relaxed that you have no desire to smoke ever again. It'll help you stop smoking."

"That's a good example," Mr. Irving said. "Now, how does it relate to a person's will-power? Will every posthypnotic suggestion work?"

Winslow raised his hand again. "Only if you *want* to follow it," he said. "For instance, if you are a very peaceful person, a hypnotist can't change you into someone who wants to start a war by giving you a posthypnotic suggestion."

"Very good," Mr. Irving told him. "That's a very important point." He picked up a piece of chalk and wrote on the blackboard, "Posthypnotic suggestion: only if you agree with it."

Mr. Irving looked around the classroom. "How does someone behave under hypnosis?" he asked.

Winslow raised his hand again. "The same as they would if they were wide awake. Maybe they're not as alert, because they're so relaxed."

Mr. Irving gave a creepy smile. "So you might be a little slower to respond? Like some kind of zombie?"

Randy and I exchanged a fast look at that. Calm down, her look said. It's just a figure of speech!

"Shall we try some hypnosis right now?" Mr. Irving asked.

"Yes!" the class shouted.

"All right, then," Mr. Irving said. "I'll need a subject." He looked around the room.

In a second every single hand was in the air. This was really interesting stuff, and every one of us wanted to be hypnotized. I did, too! Even if Mr. Irving was a little strange, I couldn't imagine anything more exciting than finding out what was in the depths of my mind!

Mr. Irving seemed a little taken aback by the

hands waving in the air. He glanced around, then looked at me. "Sabrina, why don't you come up? We'll try you under hypnosis."

I was thrilled. This was really going to be something! I went to the front of the room, where Mr. Irving had placed a chair facing away from the class. He stood in front of me, holding a pencil. Then he asked the class for complete quiet.

He turned to me. "Now, Sabrina," he began, "I can only hypnotize you with your consent. Do you want to be hypnotized?"

"Yes," I answered at once.

"All right, then. Will you look at the pencil in front of you?" He moved it slowly back and forth, and my eyes followed it. He began to talk in a soft, soothing tone of voice. "I want you to think about nothing but the pencil, nothing but the movement back and forth, back and forth. . . . You're getting tired, Sabrina. It's hard for your eyes to continue following the pencil, isn't it?"

I nodded. I *was* getting tired. I could feel my head wanting to drop down to my chest. In fact, I felt like going right to sleep in the chair, right in the middle of class.

Mr. Irving kept the pencil moving. "Do you

want to close your eyes, Sabrina? You may if you want to. But you'll hear everything I say and answer all my questions, even though you're so very tired." I closed my eyes. I didn't think I could keep them open for another second.

"All right, Sabrina. You're in a state of total relaxation. Nothing disturbs you in the least. You are open to the sound of my voice and the questions I am going to ask you." I felt limp as a doll, but when Mr. Irving talked, I couldn't seem to help but listen.

"Now, Sabrina. What is the most important thing in your life right now?"

Immediately an image of Matt sprang into my mind. "My . . . my brother," I answered. "My brother's movie."

"Your brother's movie?" asked Mr. Irving. "That sounds interesting. Why don't you tell us about this movie?"

"My brother is making a movie for the Minnesota Film Festival. I'm going to be in it. It's a horror movie called *Last Scream of the Zombies,* and my part is a girl named Andrea."

"I see," said Mr. Irving. "And is there something you want to accomplish in this movie, something you're working on now?"

I could hardly move my mouth, but the words kept coming out. It was like someone else was controlling my body. "I want to eat the right food and lose five pounds so I look the right weight in front of the camera." I thought I heard a giggle behind me, but it sounded so far away, it didn't seem to matter.

"I see," Mr. Irving's voice continued. "Is eating properly difficult for you?"

"Not . . . not exactly," I heard myself say. "But I like to eat cookies and sundaes at Fitzie's with my friends. Sometimes it's hard not to order something sweet when everybody else does."

"Yes, it is hard, Sabrina," Mr. Irving said thoughtfully. "But for you, it's going to be very easy from now on. In fact, whenever you sit down to eat, you'll find that you aren't very hungry at all. You won't have any desire for ice cream or cake or cookies. No matter what your friends are eating, you won't be tempted. You'll eat salads, skim milk, lean meats, and all kinds of vegetables. Those will become the staples of your diet."

I thought about this drowsily. No more sundaes at Fitzie's . . .

"Now, Sabrina," Mr. Irving said softly, "I'm

going to bring you out of your hypnotic state. I'm going to count to three, and when I say 'three,' you'll be wide awake and remember everything we talked about. And you will not be hungry for sweets or chocolates or ice cream. Ready? One, two, three." He clapped his hands.

I jolted awake. Mr. Irving was looking at me. "Are you all right?" he asked.

"Yes, fine," I said.

"Do you remember what we talked about?" he asked.

"Yes, Matt's movie and no junk food," I answered. I could hear laughter behind me, and when I looked around, the kids started clapping. Like undergoing hypnosis was some kind of performance or something! Well, maybe it was, in a way. "Thanks, Mr. Irving," I said. "That was very interesting."

"Thank *you*, Sabrina," he answered. "Now, for homework: I want everyone except Sabrina to write a couple of pages on the uses of hypnosis and the possible benefits and dangers it can present to the mind. Sabrina, since I've given you a posthypnotic suggestion, I want you to continue your normal activities, but please stay aware of how you feel about fattening foods.

Write down your reactions to various times and places when you usually eat. I'd like to see a few pages by Friday afternoon."

Wow! That certainly was a different kind of assignment than the ones we usually got. I even got a little excited about it. This was like keeping a specific kind of journal. It was kind of a neat way to test scientific theory, by being a sort of guinea pig.

Randy and I were still discussing hypnosis when we started walking home that day. Katie and Al were intrigued, too. "What a terrific idea for a class!" Allison exclaimed. "I'll bet everybody wished they could have been hypnotized."

"You bet," Randy told her. "Every single person wanted to go up there, but Mr. Irving didn't look at anybody until he called on Sabs."

That did seem a little odd. I also thought the idea of mind control was strange. I'd have to do more thinking about it, but right now I was more interested in getting to our first rehearsal. It was that afternoon, and I wanted to get there on time.

We turned the corner to my house, and suddenly I stopped dead. Some of the actors had already gathered in our driveway to start work, but what I noticed most was the small white car parked at the curb. It was a car I recognized very well, the one that had almost run me down a few days ago . . . in fact, the one Mr. Irving drove!

What was he doing at our house? I wondered. And did this have anything to do with the hypnosis session we'd just had?

Chapter Seven

Things were definitely getting more and more mysterious. We spent all afternoon rehearsing. Matt showed us where he wanted us to stand and move so we'd be in the camera's sight at all times. What was strange was that Mr. Irving hung around the set all through the rehearsal. Sometimes, in fact, Matt would start to give us a direction, then stop. He'd turn to Mr. Irving, and Mr. Irving would make a gesture. Then Matt would turn around and tell us to do something else. I began to wonder about this mind-control thing. Maybe Mr. Irving was practicing something like that on Matt?

I only noticed this in between rehearsing my own part, though. Andrea had a lot of lines, because she spent a lot of time hanging around the mad scientist. She was almost always there just before or after some terrible gory event occurred. Andrea was too sweet and innocent to

believe that her friend could possibly be respon-
sible for the strange behavior of the other kids.
So she never witnessed any of the bad stuff until
the big climactic scene at the very end, when she
got saved from a disgusting death by the posse.

There were a couple of scenes when I had to
do a really big scream, and I spent a lot of time
practicing that. Matt had told me he wanted the
screams to be big moments in the movie, so I
wanted to give him the best screams I could.

I decided to practice screaming twice a day,
in the morning and at night. Then I had to figure
out where I was going to do it. You can't just
walk around yelling your head off and not
expect people to notice, especially in Acorn Falls.

I finally decided that I'd get to school very
early and practice my morning screams there. At
school I wouldn't have to worry about bothering
anyone except maybe the janitor. It was a good
idea except that it meant getting up before
everybody else, which was not easy to do.

Tuesday was to be my first day of screaming
practice. I set my alarm for five o'clock. I had no
idea how I was going to drag myself out of bed
that early, but I figured it was the only chance I
had at using the bathroom in peace.

When the alarm went off, it was absolutely pitch black outside. I didn't want to wake anyone by snapping on lights all over the house, so I took a flashlight with me to the bathroom.

As quietly as I could, I crept down the stairs, shining the flashlight ahead of me. I saw a shadow on the wall by the bathroom, and my heart started to hammer.

Calm down, I told myself. It's probably just Cinnamon, our dog. She's always stalking around the house at strange hours. I made myself stand absolutely still for a few moments, until I relaxed.

As I walked around the corner, I noticed that the bathroom door was slightly open. I started toward it — and all of a sudden this huge ghost loomed up right in front of me, all in black, with this dark, horrible face!

I screamed and dropped the flashlight. The ghost flashed by me, knocking me over. That only made me scream harder.

To my surprise, instead of killing me with one blow, the ghost started screaming, too. For a minute we were both yelling at the top of our lungs while I rolled around the floor, frantically looking for the flashlight.

"What is going on down there?" my dad yelled from down the hall. But before I could tell him that it was me and that there was a demon in the house, I found the flashlight and flashed it right in the ghost's face.

Under a thick cloud of greasepaint, the ghost was Brent!

"Sabrina!" Brent gasped. "Is that you?"

"Brent! I thought you were . . ." I could hardly get the words out.

"Sabrina, what is going on down there?" I heard my dad shouting. The next thing I knew, he was standing next to me with a huge baseball bat in his hand.

"Don't, Dad, it's Brent!" I managed to croak. My voice was almost gone. That great scream I'd had no trouble with at rehearsals had just about knocked out my vocal cords! I guess it's different when you're really scared. Your whole throat closes up.

My dad snapped on the hall light, and we all stood blinking at each other in the glare.

"I'm sorry, Mr. Wells," Brent gasped. He seemed pretty shaken up, too. "Sabrina and I ran into each other in the hall, and I guess we both got a good scare."

I thought it was pretty neat of Brent. Other guys would never admit they were scared of anything. But here was Brent, who's in college, saying that he'd been scared. I thought that showed just how mature he really was. And even with all that greasepaint on, he was still one of the cutest guys I'd ever seen!

We must have looked pretty funny, because the next thing I knew, all three of us were roaring with laughter. I was in my flannel pajamas, Brent in some weird monster getup, and my dad was holding this huge bat, like some kind of modern caveman! We really looked ridiculous!

After we calmed down, my dad said, "Well, as long as you both are okay, I'm going back to bed." He headed back to his room.

Brent and I just stood looking at each other for a second. I could feel my body blush getting ready to start, and I fumbled for something to say.

"I'm going to school early," I said finally. "I want to practice for the scenes we're shooting this afternoon."

"That was my idea, too," Brent admitted sheepishly, looking down at himself. "Practicing, I mean. I also wanted to try out the makeup for the last scene."

"Well, it sure scared me," I said with a laugh, "so it must be pretty good!"

Brent laughed, too. "Tell you what," he suggested. "How about getting dressed real fast, and then we can go over our lines for today while we have breakfast?"

I thought my heart was going to burst. "Great idea," I agreed. "I'll meet you in the kitchen."

"It's a date," Brent said as he headed off toward his room.

I couldn't believe it! This great-looking hunk wanted to go over his lines with me! He really didn't have to, either, because he and Matt had plenty of time during the day to go over the scenes. But if he wanted to rehearse with me, that meant maybe he actually liked me a little.

That thought made me almost jump into the bathroom. I got cleaned up in record time and rushed upstairs to get dressed. I wanted to wear something nice, since I was going to be spending time with Brent.

I finally decided on a soft yellow sweater, which I wore over a dark blue turtleneck and dark blue leggings. It was a very simple outfit, but looked like the kind of thing Andrea might wear. And if Brent wanted to spend time with me, maybe he was beginning to see me as his best friend, the way his character thinks of Andrea in the movie.

I brushed my hair back and pinned it up with barrettes. Then I added just a tiny bit of lip gloss and ran downstairs. Brent was waiting for me in the kitchen. He had poured big bowls of cereal, popped bread in the toaster, and poured two big glasses of orange juice.

"Breakfast for our star," he teased me, indicating my place.

"Wow, this is great," I said, slipping into my chair. "I didn't know you could cook, Brent."

He smiled at me. "I'm dynamite with a toaster. And you ought to see when I really get fancy and start microwaving!"

We both laughed. Brent sat down next to me while I gulped down my juice. I wanted to be ready whenever he wanted to start rehearsing. I was so excited about rehearsing with him. I wondered if this meant he actually liked me a little more than just as actor to actor. Suddenly I wasn't hungry in the least, and somehow I didn't think it had anything to do with Mr. Irving's posthypnotic suggestion. I wanted to say something really clever and witty, but I couldn't think of a thing.

Finally I couldn't stand the silence anymore. I thought it would be smart to ask him about his ambitions, since we had so much in common. I looked down at my cereal and said, "Are you planning on being a professional monster?"

Oh, no! I thought. That's not what I meant to say at all. I could feel my entire body turning red.

But Brent laughed, as though I'd said something really witty! "Well, no," he answered, smiling. "Actually, I thought I'd try regular acting. If it doesn't work out, then maybe I'll think about being a professional monster." He smiled at me and added, "What about you? Matt says you want to be an actress."

"That's right," I admitted. "That's why I was up early today, so I could practice my screams."

"That's a good idea," Brent said. "I can see why Matt thinks so much of you."

"He does?" I asked.

"Oh, sure," Brent answered. "He told me once that for a girl your age, you were really determined and hardworking. He was sure you were going to make it. I am, too," he added.

Wow! I wasn't even sure I was really awake and hearing all this. Here was this incredible-looking guy sitting in our kitchen practically at the crack of dawn and telling me he thought I could act. This was definitely the right way to start off the day!

"Thanks, Brent," I said. "I'm sure that you're going to make it, too."

Brent just smiled and gave me the cue for our first scene together.

We did the scene twice. I knew every line perfectly, and Brent obviously noticed. When we'd finished, he said, "It's going to be a pleasure working with such a professional."

"Thanks," I said, getting up to put my cereal bowl in the sink. I didn't think I could stand many more of these compliments. I decided to clear my head by getting in some practice screams at school, just as I'd planned.

However, by the time I got to school, it was almost time for first period. It was about twenty minutes before the bell would ring, so I looked for somewhere that I could be alone. I figured the practice field would be deserted at this time of the morning, so I headed out there.

I took a quick look around but didn't see anyone, so I decided to let loose with the biggest scream I could imagine. I reared back and let it out, trying to reach the trees farthest away with the sound.

"Wow!" said a voice behind me.

Ohmygosh! Someone was listening to me scream! I turned around and looked right into the gorgeous blue eyes of Cameron Booth!

Now my body blush started again. I just couldn't stop it. I could feel myself getting red from top to bottom while I tried to think of something to say. "Hi, Cameron," was all I could come up with.

"Hi, Sabrina," Cameron said, smiling at me. "What're you doing?"

"I'm rehearsing," I said. "For my part in Matt's movie. I have to do a scream. . . ." I realized that I was starting to babble.

"Yeah," Cameron answered. "That scream is wild. We all heard you that day at the auditions. I thought you screamed just great."

That was awfully nice of him, I thought. "Thanks," I said. "I thought if I kept practicing it, it would be really good by the time I had to do it in front of the cameras."

"I don't see how it could be any better than it

was that day at the auditions," Cameron told me. I almost wanted to blush again, but this time it would have been because I was so pleased. First Brent and now Cameron. Suddenly I wished I'd read my horoscope before I came to school. I bet it said something like "This will be the best day of your entire life."

"What are you doing here?" I asked him. The practice field is awfully far away from things. Usually Cameron hangs out with his friends, just like I do.

He looked a little embarrassed. "Oh, I wanted to practice my part, too. I'm a little worried about the scene in the lab. You know, me with those beakers and things. I've never liked science much anyway, and now I'm supposed to be this guy who's crazy about it. . . . I don't know if I'm going to be very convincing."

"Sure you will," I assured him. He still looked a little uncertain, so I added, "You're a really good actor."

Cameron smiled. "Thanks, Sabrina," he said, giving me a wink. "I'll probably learn a lot just watching you work."

Wow! This was definitely turning into a memorable day. Breakfast with Brent, before school with Cameron . . . movie making was definitely my kind of job!

Chapter Eight

Randy was really getting interested in hypnosis. She checked several books out of the library and told my friends and me stories about the amazing things that hypnosis could do.

"There was this painter in Paris," she said on Thursday at lunch. "He hit a real block. He just couldn't paint anymore. He sat around for months staring at a blank canvas. After a while his friends told him about a hypnotist. So he went to see him, and after that the painter made his greatest masterpiece." Randy took a bite of her pizza and continued, "So you see, Sabs, it's more than mind control. It's also a good way of getting problems fixed."

"I don't know," I said. The more stories she told me, the more convinced I became that a good hypnotist *could* really control someone else's mind.

"Weren't you hypnotized in New York?"

Allison asked Randy.

"Yeah, I was. Sheck was, too," Randy added. Sheck was Randy's best friend when she lived in New York. "And neither of us ever had our mind controlled."

"I don't know," I said, looking down at my salad. "It all seems pretty scary to me. I mean, who knows what a really good hypnotist could do."

"Well, a good hypnotist might be able to help you do something you wanted to do. Like eat the right food," Katie said, pointing at my salad. I had to admit she had a point.

Randy picked up her tray. "I'm going to see if I can find Mr. Irving. I want to get some more information about this stuff."

We all watched her as she walked out of the cafeteria. It was totally unlike Randy to go and talk to a teacher at lunch. Usually she wanted to hang out for as long as possible.

That afternoon Mr. Irving gave us another demonstration in hypnosis. This time he asked Randy to be his subject. It must have had something to do with their lunchtime conversation. Randy was still under when the bell rang for the end of class.

Mr. Irving told the rest of us to go ahead. He said he'd bring Randy out of his hypnotic spell in a minute.

I wanted to wait for Randy, but Matt needed me in the scene he was shooting that afternoon, so I had to leave without her. As I left the room, I looked back at her over my shoulder. She looked sort of strange sitting there in a nearly empty room with this blank expression on her face.

I didn't have too long to worry about it. Today's scenes took place in one of the empty classrooms, so I changed into my costume in the girls' room. Allison and Katie waited for me as I got into the cute skirt with suspenders and lacy blouse that Matt had chosen. He said he wanted me to look as innocent and helpless as possible.

"Where's Randy?" Allison asked as I was adjusting the suspenders over my blouse.

"She's on her way," I told her. "Mr. Irving had her hypnotized when the bell rang, and he was going to bring her out of the hypnosis slowly. Besides, she's not in any scenes today."

Al looked at her watch and frowned. "But you know she loves helping out. And eighth period ended twenty minutes ago. She should be here by now."

"Maybe she's already on the set," Katie suggested.

"That's right," I reassured Allison. "Maybe she's helping with the lights or something."

But when we got to the classroom where Matt had set up his equipment, there was no sign of Randy at all.

"Hi, kids," Matt called. "Come on over. Let's get going."

Brent was already there and in costume. He was wearing a white lab coat that reminded me a lot of Mr. Irving's. "Hi, Sabrina." He smiled. "Ready for our scene?"

"Hi, Brent," I said, smiling back at him. "Sure. I'm all set." I saw Cameron out of the corner of my eye and gave him a little wave before turning back to Brent. After all, I did have a job to do, no matter how cute Cameron was. Besides, he was also there to do a job.

"Have you seen Randy yet?" Katie whispered to me. She definitely sounded worried. I began to worry, too. Why had Mr. Irving wanted to keep her after class?

Just then Matt called, "Brent! Sabrina! Places."

"I've got to go," I told Katie. "Look, if Randy

doesn't come in soon, let's run down and see if she's still in the science room, okay?"

Matt told Brent and me what he wanted us to do and watched us run through the scene once. Then he said, "Okay, let's go for a take. Quiet on the set. Ready, sound rolling, and . . . action!"

I walked in the door of the classroom and spoke to Brent. He answered just the way he was supposed to, and soon I was walking out the door again. The whole thing took maybe a minute at the most.

"Cut!" called Matt. "Very good! We'll print that. Now let's do the close-ups of both of you."

As they switched off the big overhead lights, I noticed Mr. Irving come in quietly. There was no sign of Randy, though. I wanted to ask Mr. Irving if he knew where she was, but he immediately caught Matt's arm and began whispering to him. Matt stopped what he was doing and listened carefully. Something about that made me very nervous.

"Come on," I said to Katie and Allison. "Let's go see if we can find Randy. I don't know why she's not here."

"But they're shooting your close-up in just a minute," Katie reminded me.

But I had learned something about movie making in the last few days. "It's okay, Katie," I said. "It'll take them a while to set things up. We've got plenty of time. Let's go."

Quickly Katie, Allison, and I hurried out the door and down the stairs to Mr. Irving's room. I almost hoped Randy wasn't there. Something awful was beginning to nag at the back of my mind, and I was almost afraid to say the thought out loud.

The classroom was empty. Randy wasn't there. But there *was* something familiar lying on one of the desks. It was Randy's Walkman, which she carries everywhere with her.

"That's funny," Allison said, puzzled. "How could Randy forget her Walkman?"

"You'd think it was attached to her by an umbilical cord," Katie agreed. "It does seem strange that she left it here."

I looked at the Walkman closely. There was a tape inside it. It was just a plain white tape with no label on it at all. Something dreadful started to bubble at the back of my mind. I remembered all the stories about hypnotists that Randy had been telling me.

"Just a second, guys," I said, slipping on

Randy's headphones. "I want to listen to a little of this."

I pressed the PLAY button. I think I knew that I'd hear Mr. Irving's voice. It sounded just like it had when he spoke softly and quietly to hypnotize me. "All right, Randy," Mr. Irving said, "close your eyes and imagine my pencil in front of your face. Nothing else, just my pencil. Your eyes follow it slowly, back and forth, back and forth . . . until your eyes start to feel heavy. You want to go to sleep."

Oh, no! I could hardly believe it! Mr. Irving was using a tape to hypnotize Randy!

Quickly I turned off the tape before *I* got hypnotized again. "Maybe he really is a mad scientist," I said in a hushed voice.

"What are you talking about?" Katie asked.

Quickly I explained my suspicions. "It all makes sense, guys. He hypnotized me to find out the details about Matt's movie, then he hypnotized Randy. What's worse, he gave her a tape so he can control her even when he's not around!"

"Do you think that's really true?" Allison asked.

"Yes!" I said desperately. "He's done something terrible to Randy. Maybe he's even trying to turn her into a zombie!"

"But she left the tape here," Katie pointed out, "so he can't have complete control of her mind yet."

"I'm still not sure, Sabs. Look at you," Allison added. "He hypnotized you, and he didn't try to control you."

Maybe that was true. Then I remembered lunch in the cafeteria. "He is controlling me!" I yelled. "What did I eat for lunch today? Salad and raspberry seltzer — when it was pizza day in the cafeteria!"

"So? Isn't that what you wanted to do?" Katie asked.

"It's what he told me to do!" I said. "When he hypnotized me, he told me I wouldn't have any craving for junk food, no matter what my friends ate. You all ate pizza and brownies today, and I didn't even want any of it! Does that sound normal to you?" I asked indignantly.

"No, Sabs." Katie laughed. "Considering what you usually eat, that's definitely weird."

"But it seems like a healthy impulse," Allison added. "And since you really want to eat right anyway, maybe he did you a big favor."

I could see that Katie and Allison weren't going to be convinced by my theory unless I came up with a lot more evidence, and fast. But I was sure, in my mind, that Mr. Irving was real trouble. It had something to do with Matt and his movie, and I was absolutely determined to find out what. Otherwise, I had a sinking feeling Bradley Junior High could end up with zombies for students!

Chapter Nine

At dinner that night my mom served her famous spaghetti, which I've always loved. Usually I can eat at least two helpings, but tonight when I looked at it, it didn't appeal to me at all. I couldn't imagine why I'd ever wanted to eat it.

That's Mr. Irving's doing, I told myself grimly. Well, I was going to show him that I could resist his mind control. "Pass the spaghetti, please," I requested.

Sam hooted. "Hey, Sabs, I thought you were eating healthy during the shoot," he taunted me.

"Spaghetti is very healthy," I informed him, ladling out pasta onto my plate.

"That's great, but would you mind leaving some for the rest of us?" Luke asked.

I looked down at my plate. I had spooned out an awful lot. So what? I'll eat it all, I told myself defiantly. This was resisting mind control not breaking a diet.

My mom looked up from the salad she was dishing out. "Cut it out, Luke," she told him. "If Sabrina's hungry, she can eat as much as she likes."

"Thanks, Mom," I said gratefully. I reached for the plate of garlic bread and picked up the biggest piece.

I really wanted to dig right in and eat, but somehow I just couldn't bring myself to do it. I really wasn't interested in any of the food except Mom's salad, which tasted just delicious. I ate a whole plateful and dished out a big second helping. So far, though, I hadn't eaten a mouthful of my spaghetti or the garlic bread.

"Hey, Sabs, is something wrong?" Matt asked. "Aren't you feeling well?"

"Sure," I answered. "I feel great. Why?"

Matt pointed his fork at the untouched spaghetti on my plate. "Are you waiting for the Tooth Fairy to come and eat it?"

I was embarrassed, but I was also determined to break through Mr. Irving's hypnotic spell and help Randy. I wondered what Mr. Irving had programmed her to do.

Then it occurred to me. Maybe Mr. Irving

was trying to sabotage Matt's movie. The outlines of his horrible plan were forming in my brain. I just had to figure out how Randy fit into the whole thing. I suppose she could get in the way of the rest of the technical crew. She was helping out with a lot of the off-screen stuff.

Now I had *really* lost my appetite. The thought of Randy messing up the lights or the cameras was just awful. And if Mr. Irving had told her to do it in a hypnotic trance, she might not even realize what she was doing. Poor Randy, I thought. She might not even realize that her mind was being controlled.

It was up to me to save her and everybody else at Bradley. Filled with determination, I took a huge forkful of the cooling spaghetti. As soon as that was down, I took another. And another. Soon I had eaten the entire plate.

"Dessert, anybody?" my mom asked. "I baked Death by Chocolate." She brought in a fabulous chocolate cake with a big bowl of whipped cream next to it. Usually I can't resist Mom's Death by Chocolate, no matter how I vowed to diet. Tonight I had no appetite for it at all, even to taste it. But I was determined to get the best of the hypnosis. I wasn't going to let a delicious chocolate dessert get by me! I ate two whole helpings *with* whipped cream — even though I thought I was going to burst halfway through.

After dinner Matt and Brent rushed off to the garage, where they'd set up a little editing bay to edit each day's footage. I wanted to go with them so I could see my performance. But I decided it was more important to reach Randy, if I could.

I dialed Randy's number, and her mother picked up. "Hi, Mrs. . . . I mean, Olivia," I said. "It's Sabrina." Randy's mother always asks us to call her by her first name. Sometimes it's hard to remember that. I almost always want to slip and say Mrs. Zak.

"Hello, Sabrina," Olivia answered. She didn't sound upset at all for a woman whose daughter might be a walking zombie. "How's the movie going? Randy's so excited about it."

"It's going great, Olivia," I answered. "Could I please speak to Randy? It's kind of important."

"I'm sorry, Sabrina, she's not here," Olivia replied.

Not at home? I thought I was going to start crying right then and there. Mr. Irving couldn't have her out in some dark graveyard or something, could he? Shouldn't Olivia be at least a little worried about her?

"Do you know where she is?" I asked, trying not to panic.

"She's at Winslow Barton's house," Olivia answered. "She went over to use his music-composing software. You could call her there. Or I'll ask her to call you when she gets home."

"No, that's all right," I said. "Thanks, Olivia." I hung up and tried to figure things out. If Randy was with Winslow, she had to be all right. Or at least she must have seemed all right on the surface. Maybe if you don't know somebody's under a hypnotic spell, they seem perfectly normal to you. I really didn't know what someone in a hypnotic spell would act like.

I thought I'd better check out this hypnosis business. I should have listened to Randy's stories more carefully. If I knew more about hypnosis, maybe I'd be able to help her. But who could I talk to about it? Who wouldn't think I was completely nuts?

Matt! Matt had written a whole movie about a mad scientist and mind control. He probably researched the subject before he wrote his script.

I'll ask Matt, I decided. I just won't say a word to him about Mr. Irving. For some reason, Matt seemed to get a real kick out of having Mr. Irving around. As far as I could see, Mr. Irving didn't have anything to do with making the movie, but Matt was always asking his advice and listening to his suggestions.

Of course, Mr. Irving could be controlling Matt's mind, too, I thought, shuddering. No. I won't think about anything negative. I just have to get some information.

I went into the garage where Matt and Brent were bent over their little editing machine. Matt had his script open on his lap.

"Four frames, three, two —" Brent called out.

"Mark it at two," Matt said, not looking up from the script. Brent took a thick pencil of some sort and made some marks on the film. Then he noticed me and gave me a big smile.

"Hi, Sabrina," he said warmly. "Did you come to watch us edit your performance?"

"Well, not exactly," I said. "Not tonight. Matt, could I ask you a question?"

Matt looked at me. I must have looked pretty upset, because he pulled up an empty chair next to him. "Okay, babe, sit down. What's the problem?"

I felt a little nervous. I didn't want to talk about mind control in front of Brent. He'd probably think I was crazy.

Brent must have seen how I felt, because he got up and stretched. "I think I'll take a break. I'll be back in ten minutes."

He strolled out, and Matt looked at me. I couldn't think of any tactful way to say it, so finally I blurted it out. "Matt, what do you know about mind control?"

Matt stared at me. "Mind control?"

"Like the hypnosis in your script. The mad scientist hypnotizing these kids to turn them into zombies. I'm very interested," I finished lamely. I didn't want to mention that I was afraid Randy might be a zombie.

Matt whistled. He knew this wasn't exactly a casual question. Either he was a very good director who knew when an actress was lying, or he'd been my older brother too long.

Matt looked hard at me. I guess he could tell that I wanted to keep the *real* reasons for my questions a secret. Finally he just smiled. "Okay, if it's research for your part, fire away."

"Well, for instance," I began, glad that he had

bought my excuse, "suppose Andrea found out that the mad scientist was doing this stuff. She noticed some of her friends acting strange, but she didn't know why. What would be some of the symptoms she'd notice?"

"But Andrea doesn't notice anything," Matt pointed out. "That's not in the script."

"Matt, just suppose it was!" I was getting really mad now. Here I was trying to save the *brain* and possibly the *life* of one of my best friends, and Matt was arguing with me over tiny details.

Matt grinned. "Okay. What would she notice? I don't know . . . maybe her friends would be acting a little spacey. You know, she would talk to them and they wouldn't hear her, or maybe they'd seem a little distant. Maybe they would spend less time with her and more time alone. Maybe they'd be tired all the time. Stuff like that. Is that what you want to know?"

I was getting really excited. So far, it sounded like I was on the right track. I hadn't been able to talk to Randy yet, but that hypnosis tape in her Walkman had to be a sign of something. I wished I'd brought the tape home with me to listen to all the way through. But Allison had taken it with her to drop off at Randy's house on her way home. By now, maybe Randy had listened to it again and again. She might be completely under Mr. Irving's spell!

"How would I — I mean Andrea — know when somebody was completely a zombie?" I asked.

Matt laughed. "Sabs, there's no such thing as a zombie. Like there's no such thing as a ghost."

"There have to be zombies," I insisted. "If you can use hypnosis to control somebody, there have to be people who are completely under someone else's control."

Matt gave me a hug. "Sabs, zombies are an old idea. Long ago, people thought they could curse their enemies by putting voodoo spells on them. They made funny little dolls and stuck pins in them, and that was supposed to hurt or kill the people they wanted to harm. Or it could change them into zombies with no free will. But these are just superstitions."

"But if you believed it, it could kill you, right?" I asked.

"Well . . . if you believed it, yes, I *guess* it could," Matt said dubiously.

Randy certainly believed it. I sighed and looked

at the film in the editing machine. I knew that pretty soon it would be a real movie and hopefully lots of people would come and see it.

"Matt," I asked suddenly, "what happens if your movie wins first place at the festival?"

Matt grinned. "Well, then it gets shown all over the country. Thousands and thousands of people will see it, and you'll probably end up famous."

At any other time that thought would have thrilled me. Me, a famous star of the screen! Now, though, I thought about thousands of people seeing the movie. Maybe Mr. Irving didn't want anyone seeing Matt's movie, because it was just too close to real life. Maybe he had to stop Matt so he could carry out his plan for changing students into zombies without interference. Maybe Randy was his first zombie, and he was using her to destroy the movie.

Matt looked down at the script on his lap. "Was any of that helpful for your research?" he asked.

"Yes," I said, getting up from the chair. "Thanks, Matt." All the pieces were beginning to come together. I knew I had a real problem on my hands. I had to save Randy — and the movie!

Chapter Ten

Sabrina calls Randy.

OLIVIA: Hello?

SABRINA: Hello, Olivia? This is Sabrina again.

OLIVIA: Hello, Sabrina. How are you?

SABRINA: Oh, I'm still fine, thank you. Did Randy come home yet? Can I talk to her?

OLIVIA: I'm sorry, Sabrina. Randy came home a little while ago and said she was very tired. She looked exhausted, so I told her to go right to bed. She's probably sound asleep by now. Can it wait until the morning?

SABRINA: I hope so, Olivia. Did Randy seem at all, you know, different? A little strange?

OLIVIA: Why, no, Sabrina. Just quiet. She

93

might be getting the flu, if that's what you mean. It's going around, you know.

SABRINA: Yeah, that's true. Thanks, Olivia. I guess I'll see Randy in school tomorrow.

OLIVIA: Sure, Sabrina. Good night.

SABRINA: Good night, Olivia.

Sabrina calls Katie.

EMILY: Hello, Campbell and Beauvais residence. Emily speaking.

SABRINA: Emily? This is Sabrina. Can I —

EMILY: Hi, Sabrina. How's the movie going? I guess all that early morning practicing helped, huh? Katie told me you got the biggest part.

SABRINA: The movie's great. Please, Emily, this is a real emergency. Could I talk to Katie right away?

EMILY: Well, she's taking a shower right now. I don't think she can come to the phone.

SABRINA: Please! It's superimportant!

EMILY: Well, hold on. I'll see if I can get her to the phone.

EMILY: Katie, Sabrina's on the phone for
            you! She says it's an emergency!

(Katie picks up the phone.)
KATIE: Hello? Sabs? What's wrong?
SABRINA: Oh, Katie, we are in such trouble!
            Especially Randy!
KATIE: Why, what's the matter? What's
            wrong with Randy?
SABRINA: I finally figured it out! The whole
            mind-control thing! Mr. Irving's
            trying to sabotage Matt's movie by
            controlling Randy's mind!
KATIE: *What?*
SABRINA: You know, so she'll mess up the
            movie without even realizing
            what she's doing. That way, he can
            turn the kids at Bradley into zom-
            bies, and nobody'll ever know.
KATIE: Sabs, how do you know? This
            sounds a little farfetched. Why
            would Mr. Irving want to turn stu-
            dents into zombies?
SABRINA: Look, he's already got Randy
            under his spell. I called her twice
            tonight. First, her mother said she

was at Winslow's house working on his musical software program. The second time, she said Randy was already asleep, and it's only eight o'clock!

KATIE: Maybe she was tired.

SABRINA: That's what Olivia said. She also said Randy looked strange, so she told her to go to sleep early. I talked to Matt, and he told me all those symptoms were signs of somebody becoming a zombie!

KATIE: A zombie! Randy?

SABRINA: Look, I know it sounds crazy, but a lot of things sound crazy at first. We've got to stop Mr. Irving right away! We've got to figure out how to release Randy from his mind control so she doesn't become a zombie. I can't do this by myself, Katie! I need your help.

KATIE: Okay, I'm convinced. What we need is a real plan. Why don't you talk to Allison? If I don't dry off, I'm going to catch pneumonia standing out here.

SABRINA:	That's a great idea, Katie. I'll call Allison, and then we can talk it over later.
KATIE:	Great. Good luck, Sabs.
SABRINA:	Thanks. Bye!
KATIE:	Bye.

Sabrina calls Allison.

ALLISON:	Good evening, Cloud residence.
SABRINA:	Allison! Is that you?
ALLISON:	Yes . . . Sabrina? Is that you? You sound terrible.
SABRINA:	Allison, I just talked to Katie. We've got to come up with a plan fast to save Randy's brain from Mr. Irving.
ALLISON:	*What?*
SABRINA:	He's using mind control on Randy, to get her to sabotage Matt's movie so he can turn all the students at Bradley into zombies. We've got to stop him!
ALLISON:	Are you sure, Sabrina? Do you really think Mr. Irving is a mad scientist?
SABRINA:	Yes, I'm certain of it. And Katie is,

too. You've got to help us figure
out what to do before it's too late.

ALLISON: We can't do it on our own . . .
nobody would believe us. But if
we got proof somehow, then we
could take the proof to some
adults and ask them to step in
and stop Mr. Irving.

SABRINA: That's a great idea, Allison!

ALLISON: We'll need a camera, and we'll
need to follow Mr. Irving around
when he doesn't know we're
there.

SABRINA: Well, we can't do it during the
day, because we're all in class.

ALLISON: What about after class? Doesn't
he stay late to work in the lab in
the afternoon? We could catch
him then.

SABRINA: What if he doesn't do anything in
all that time that's weird?

ALLISON: Well, we may just have to come
back at night, then. That's when
we might really get some incrim-
inating evidence.

SABRINA: I wish you'd stop using those

big words, Al!

ALLISON: I mean, we'll get pictures that will convince our parents and maybe Mr. Hansen that Mr. Irving's doing something sinister. Then they can confront him and make him stop.

SABRINA: I knew you'd think of something! That sounds great, Al!

ALLISON: Okay. I'll borrow my mother's camera and bring it to school tomorrow. And we'd better keep quiet about this. We don't want to tip off Mr. Irving about what we're doing.

SABRINA: Right. This is a hush-hush operation all the way.

ALLISON: Okay, then. You tell Katie, and I'll see you both in school tomorrow. If Randy's really in trouble, we'll find out then.

SABRINA: Thanks for figuring out the plan, Al. It's going to work great.

ALLISON: See you tomorrow, Sabs.

SABRINA: See you, Al.

Chapter Eleven

I kept looking for Randy all Friday morning, but in homeroom I found out that she hadn't come to school at all. Katie, Allison, and I exchanged significant looks when Ms. Staats marked her absent. I would have been really depressed if Allison hadn't shown us the camera she'd borrowed from her mom. She showed it to us at her locker just before homeroom. I knew that with the camera we would get whatever we needed to stop all this weirdness at Bradley once and for all.

That afternoon I noticed that Mr. Irving wasn't hanging around the set at school. At least I didn't see him while I was doing my scenes. On one hand, I was relieved, but on the other, I was really scared. It bothered me that he would disappear on the same day as Randy.

Cameron was getting ready to do a scene. I wanted to stay and watch, and maybe encourage him, but Katie and Allison were giving me "hurry up" looks. I followed them out.

"Let's go outside," Katie suggested. "We don't want Mr. Irving to see us running around the halls."

So we sneaked out the door and doubled back to the window outside Mr. Irving's room. Mr. Irving was inside, doing something that looked really strange. He was standing in front of maybe twenty kids, all of them actors in Matt's movie. In his softest voice, he commanded, "All right, three paces to the right . . . three paces to the left."

Sure enough, as soon as he spoke, the kids shuffled to the right and then to the left, all of them looking absolutely glassy-eyed. I even saw Stacy the Great and Eva Malone, eyes staring and wide, taking stiff little steps to the right and the left. It looked really gruesome!

"Ohmygosh," I whispered. "Look at that! He's already got them under his spell!"

Allison quickly pointed her camera at the scene and took several quick pictures. "Got it," she assured me.

Katie looked thoughtfully into the classroom. "I don't know, Al," she said. "Look at them. If you show somebody a picture of this, it'll just look like a teacher leading a class."

"You're right," I wailed. "Even if we know what's going on, it won't convince anybody else."

"What'll we do?" Allison asked, sounding concerned.

I tried to sound as confident as possible. "We'll just have to come back tonight," I announced. "He'll probably be working in the lab, as usual."

Katie and Allison looked a little nervous. To tell the truth, I wasn't feeling so great about it, either. Usually it's Randy who keeps up our nerve for something like this. It would be tough sneaking back to school in the dark without her.

"Come on, guys," I said, trying to encourage my friends. "We've got to do this for Randy. If we don't, she could end up being a bubble brain for the rest of her life!"

"That's true," Katie agreed, her voice quavering a little. Then she said firmly, "I'll be here."

"Me too," Allison agreed.

"Great," I told them. "Let's meet at my house at seven-thirty."

By seven-fifteen I was all set. Katie and

Allison came over at seven-thirty.

"Boy, am I glad to see you guys," I said to them. "Now all we have to do is get to school without being noticed and see what Mr. Irving's up to."

"I brought flashbulbs for the camera," Allison told me, patting one of her pockets.

"Great idea," Katie said. "But be careful not to use one until you're sure you've got a great picture. We may only get one chance to use it, because Mr. Irving would see a flashbulb going off and probably try to follow us."

The thought of that made me feel a little sick. I wondered if he'd followed Randy home yesterday. I'd called her house again when I got home from school, but Olivia told me this time she had a slight case of the flu and was asleep in her room. Now I was determined to stop Mr. Irving once and for all. He wasn't going to get away with controlling the minds of Bradley Junior High students if I could help it!

"Let's go, everybody!" I said finally. I called to my mom, "Mom, we're going to talk a short walk. Okay?"

"Fine," Mom called back. "But don't stay out too long."

"That's okay," I assured her. "We'll hurry back."

"We'll definitely hurry," Katie said when we were outside. "Especially if Mr. Irving sees us." She shivered slightly. "It almost feels like someone's following us already."

"Don't say that," Allison pleaded as we hurried toward school. "I feel strange enough about this as it is."

"I wish it wasn't foggy again," I moaned. "I just hate fog. It's so spooky."

"At least there's a full moon," Katie pointed out. "It's a little easier to see, anyway."

"That makes it even spookier," I said. We were almost at school.

"Look!" Allison whispered. "There's a light on, on the ground floor!"

We all looked. Sure enough, the only light on in the entire building was in Mr. Irving's lab. I looked grimly at my friends. "Okay," I said, feeling like a general. "It's now or never. This is for Randy, right?"

"Right," we all chorused together. That made me feel better, like I had comrades-in-arms, or whatever those adventure movies call them.

As we slowly moved toward Mr. Irving's

window, I thought I heard something behind me. Oh, no! Had someone discovered us already?

I turned around and saw a dark figure. I was terrified. I opened my mouth to scream, but the figure grabbed me and clamped a hand over my mouth. Now I was really scared. Whoever it was was taller and stronger than I. We rolled on the ground for a minute, until Allison shined her pocket flashlight right in our faces.

"Randy!" Allison gasped.

"In person," Randy said, still clamping her hand over my mouth. "You okay now, Sabs, or are you going to yell?"

I shook my head, still trying to see. Allison lifted the flashlight so I could see Randy's face. Randy was wearing what looked like this slinky black turtleneck cat suit. Even though I was still pretty shaky, I could tell it was the coolest thing I'd ever seen. "I'm fine," I said.

Then I remembered that there was a very good chance that Randy was a zombie. I'd better make sure that it's really Randy I'm talking to, I thought.

"What are you doing here?" I whispered to the person who seemed to be Randy. "Olivia said you were asleep with the flu."

Randy shrugged. When she did that, she looked just like herself. "Oh, I was feeling a lot better when I woke up," she said. "I called your house and your mother said you were having Katie and Al over, so I figured it was okay to come over, too. But when I got there, you were all leaving. So I followed you. What are you doing here?"

"Spying on Mr. Irving," Katie blurted out. "He's been controlling the minds of the students in Matt's movie, and —" She stopped and bit her lip.

Nobody wanted to mention to Randy that we were afraid her mind was being controlled, too. She sounded just like herself, though. In fact, she sounded perfectly normal. Was it possible that Mr. Irving's mind control hadn't worked on her?

"Why are you spying on him?" Randy asked. "He's a really neat guy. We had a really cool talk yesterday after school."

"You mean after he hypnotized you?" I asked.

"Sabs, I asked him to," Randy explained. "Remember when I told you about that painter? I decided to ask Mr. Irving to hypnotize me so that I could write songs on Winslow's music-software program. So he did. It was great. I spent most of the afternoon yesterday working at Winslow's house. I wrote the neatest song."

I could feel my body blush coming on, even if it was completely dark and nobody else could see it. So that's what Randy was doing — songwriting? She wasn't under a hypnotic spell?

"You mean Mr. Irving wasn't trying to control your mind?" Allison asked.

"Of course not," Randy said patiently. "But he agreed with me that hypnosis could help enhance your talents, so I asked him to try it. It really worked. He even gave me a tape to help me hypnotize myself whenever I want to write again. The only problem is, you get so tired. Songwriting is definitely hard work."

I could see Katie and Allison looking at me. I knew they were no longer completely convinced that Mr. Irving was a mad scientist. "Well, let's look anyway," I said. "I know I saw a beaker of blood in the lab, and that hand in the trunk of his car. Just because he wasn't trying to control Randy's mind doesn't mean he isn't a mad scientist. Let's keep going."

Katie and Allison exchanged glances. "Well, I guess we could take a look," Katie said hesitantly. "I mean, as long as we've come all this way."

We all crowded together to peer through the window of Mr. Irving's lab. It was easy to see him, since the room was lit up. He was measuring out a yellow powder from a jar and dropping it carefully into a test tube, which was held with a metal clamp over a Bunsen burner. As he dropped the powder into the test tube, the whole mixture inside bubbled up thick and red.

"Blood!" I whispered. "What did I tell you?"

Katie nudged Allison. "Quick! Get a picture!" she said urgently.

Allison took out her camera and aimed it at the test tube. Just then Mr. Irving moved right in front of it, blocking her view.

"We really need a picture of that test tube," I told Allison. "That'll be the real proof."

Allison kept her camera ready, but Mr. Irving was doing something with the test tube. When he finally moved away, we saw that he'd turned off the Bunsen burner and was carrying the mixture in a beaker. Just when Allison had the camera aimed right at the beaker, though, Mr. Irving turned off the light and left the room!

"Oh, no!" I cried out. "He's leaving!"

"We've got to follow him," Randy said grimly. "Come on! He'll be coming out the side door!"

She sounded just like her old self, which made me feel a lot better as we all hurried after her. At least Mr. Irving hadn't destroyed Randy's brain. She was still the same wonderful person she'd always been.

Suddenly it seemed as though he was coming right at us. Randy pulled us all back into the bushes. I guess Mr. Irving was either very focused on his beaker or unable to see that well at night, because he walked right past us. He was heading in the direction we'd come.

Randy waited until he'd gone a little distance, then signaled us to follow. Keeping silent, we trailed him out to the street. He walked so briskly that we had to hurry just to keep up. In a few minutes, though, I started getting worried all over again. Mr. Irving seemed to be headed straight for my house!

We all gasped when he walked right up the front steps of my house and rang the doorbell. Matt opened the door and said loudly, "Mr. Irving! I'm so glad to see you! Come right in."

"Matt, I think I've got it," we heard Mr. Irving say. Then the door closed behind him.

"We've got to stop him," I said. I had terrible visions of Matt's becoming a zombie by drinking zombie blood or something. I couldn't let Mr. Irving do that to my favorite brother!

Completely forgetting about caution, I ran toward the house. Randy, Allison, and Katie were right behind me.

We burst into the hall. Matt was holding the beaker up to the light and saying, "That's really amazing. I never expected anything like this."

"Matt, don't drink that!" I screamed. "It's zombie blood! Stop!"

. I ran over and tried to grab the beaker. Matt pulled it away from me. "Sabrina, what are you doing? Leave this alone!"

"He's trying to control your mind!" I pleaded with him. "Don't drink it. You'll be under his control forever!"

Matt looked shocked. "Sabs, calm down. This is Tennessee Irving, the special-effects wizard. He did all the great blood scenes in Reginald Hatch's movies. He's been trying out a new type of fake blood for my movie. It's going to work really well with the kind of film we're using."

"For your movie . . ." I stared at the beaker. "You mean that's not blood?"

Mr. Irving laughed. "Definitely not, Sabrina. But I'm very flattered if you thought it was. That means audiences will think it's real, too. That's my job."

"This was all for special effects?" I asked, trying to sort out my thoughts. "You mean you weren't trying to control the minds of the Bradley students?"

Now Matt and Mr. Irving were both laughing. I was beginning to feel really dumb. "If I can't do it as a teacher," Mr. Irving assured me, "I doubt I'd ever be able to manage it, even as a mad scientist. Is that what you were afraid I was?"

I hated to answer, but I wanted to be truthful. "I guess maybe I got a little carried away," I said finally. "I mean, we were making this movie about zombies and mad scientists — and I saw you with all those students giving them directions about how to move."

"That was your brother's doing, Sabrina," Mr. Irving said. "He asked me to rehearse the students in the zombie scenes while he was doing other things. I was just directing them, the way he would have if he'd had the time."

"My sister's got a very vivid imagination,"

Matt explained, ruffling my hair. "Sometimes she doesn't quite get the connection between reality and fantasy."

Suddenly I was mad. It was true that I had a vivid imagination, but it was also true that I hadn't imagined that hand sticking out of the trunk of Mr. Irving's car. "Uh, Mr. Irving, about that day you almost hit me with your car . . ."

"Ah, yes, Sabrina. I am sorry about that," Mr. Irving assured me.

"Thank you. But I noticed something in your trunk. It was a . . . a hand." I tried to be casual about this, but my knees were trembling.

Mr. Irving threw back his head and laughed. "That was Gwendolyn. My favorite plastic corpse."

"Plastic corpse?" I repeated as the others burst into laughter.

"Yes, she's one of my favorite special effects," Mr. Irving explained. "We put her on the ground covered with fake blood, and she looks just like a real girl who's been disposed of. Mr. Hatch uses her in his movies all the time."

For a minute I really felt dumb. Then I decided not to worry about it. After all, nobody had gotten hurt. Best of all, Matt wasn't in danger.

And, with Mr. Irving's help, it looked like his movie was going to be just great!

Chapter Twelve

"Wow, listen to that applause!" Randy whispered as we watched the end of Matt's movie. "Everybody's crazy about it."

"Look at the judges," Katie said, nudging me. "They're all nodding at each other."

My parents, my brothers, my friends, and I were sitting in box seats at the Minnesota Film Festival. We'd come for the screening of *Last Scream of the Zombies*, which Matt had finished and sent in to the festival. Now we just had to wait for the results. Matt was so nervous that his skin was dead white. Mr. Irving, sitting next to him, looked very serious.

Personally, I thought the movie was fabulous. It was absolutely awesome to see myself up on the big screen. Whenever I screamed in the movie, there was a murmur from the audience, so I guess they liked it. The rest of the film was great, too. Cameron had turned in a fine performance. I wondered if he'd ever thought about becoming a professional actor. Stacy the Great, who'd bragged all over school about being so important in the film, appeared for maybe a minute and a half, total. But I had to admit that she was really good.

Finally the judges got up to announce the winners in the horror category. As we heard the names of the runners-up being read, I saw Matt's face getting whiter and whiter. Finally they got to the grand prize. "First place goes to a film of great imagination by a young director," one of the judges announced. "That film is . . . *Last Scream of the Zombies* by Matthew Wells!"

We all yelled like crazy and applauded as Matt stood up. He walked up to the judges, shook their hands, and accepted his award. He was even personally congratulated by Reginald Hatch himself. Katie, Randy, Al, and I hugged each other ecstatically. This was definitely one of the big moments of my life!

After the awards, we walked out into the lobby. Matt had to stop every few feet to thank the people who congratulated him. He looked incredibly happy.

Just then a man touched my arm. "Excuse me,

are you Sabrina Wells?" he asked.

"Yes, I'm Sabrina," I said, wondering what he wanted.

He pulled out a business card and handed it to me. "My name is Jeff Fields," he explained. "I'm in advertising with the Campion Company, and we're representing Riddance Roach Spray. We're going to be doing some radio spots featuring a woman screaming. I was really impressed with your scream, Sabrina. Do you think you'd want to do it for us in a roach-spray commercial?"

I stood still, absolutely stunned. I was totally speechless. This is my big break, I told myself. My first step into the world of professional acting. Screaming in a roach-spray commercial sounded great to me!

"I'd love to," I said, regaining my voice. I was holding on to his card for dear life. "Thanks."

"Fine," said Mr. Fields. "Why don't you call me next week, and we'll talk over the details and set up the taping." He gave me a smile and walked away.

Allison, Randy, and Katie came up behind me. "Sabs, who was that?" Katie asked. "He looked really important."

"He was," I said slowly. "In fact, I think it may be the most important thing that ever happened to me."

"Oh, no, not again!" Randy moaned. "Last time, that meant following mad scientists with beakers of blood!"

"What did he want?" Katie asked.

I grinned and looked around. There were very few people left in the lobby, so I really wasn't going to bother anyone. I took a deep breath and —

"Aaaeeeeeeeeeeeeeeeeeeee!"

Don't Miss
Girl Talk #32
KATIE'S CLOSE CALL

My whole body felt heavy and tired as I looked through blurry eyes at the walls of the hospital room.

It was still Wednesday evening, or at least, I thought it was. I wasn't really sure, because when I first got to the hospital, the doctor had given me medicine that had made me really sleepy. I figured it was evening, anyway, since I could see through the half-closed blinds in my hospital room that it was dark out.

The room was empty except for my bed, a chair, a TV hung high on the wall, and a small table next to my bed with a phone on it. Looking around it, I wondered where Mom was. I kind of remembered opening my eyes before and seeing her sitting in the chair, but maybe it was just a dream.

As I shifted to sit up a little, I felt a pinching sensation in my arm. Glancing down, I saw that there was a needle in my left arm. It led to a soft bag half-filled with clear liquid that was hanging from a metal hook above my head. I wrinkled my nose and looked away.

Yuck! I didn't like the idea of the I.V. being stuck in my arm at all. I would definitely have to try not to look at it again.

I forgot all about the I.V. a second later, when I heard Mom's muffled voice coming from outside my room. "Dr. Stone, when will you be able to operate?" she asked.

The doctor was speaking so softly that I couldn't make out much of anything. Her monotone, technical-sounding voice came through the door in bits and pieces.

". . . the infection . . . a rupture . . . fatal . . . immediate surgery . . . wait until Katie's fever breaks . . ."

I blinked as my stepbrother, Michel, appeared in the doorway, carrying an overnight bag. He rushed over to me and sat on the edge of the bed, holding my hand. My sister, Emily, was right behind him. She came over to my other side and gently pushed a stray strand of hair out of my face. "It's going to be all right," she said softly. "I promise!"

"But the doctor said it's . . . fatal!" I sobbed.

TALK BACK!
TELL US WHAT YOU THINK ABOUT
GIRL TALK BOOKS

Name _____

Address _____

City _____ State _____ Zip_____

Birthday _____ Mo._____ Year _____

Telephone Number (____)_____

1) Did you like this GIRL TALK book?

Check one: YES_____ NO_____

2) Would you buy another Girl Talk book?

Check one: YES_____ NO_____

If you like GIRL TALK books, please answer questions 3-5;
otherwise go directly to question 6.

3) What do you like most about GIRL TALK books?

Check one: Characters_____Situations_____
           Telephone Talk_____Other_____

4) Who is your favorite GIRL TALK character?

Check one: Sabrina_____ Katie_____ Randy_____
Allison_____ Stacy_____ Other (give name) _____

5) Who is your *least* favorite character?

_____

6) Where did you buy this GIRL TALK book?

Check one: Bookstore____Toy store____Discount store____
Grocery store___Supermarket___Other (give name)_____

Please turn over to continue survey.

7) How many GIRL TALK books have you read?

Check one: 0____   1 to 2____   3 to 4 ____   5 or more____

8) In what type of store would you look for GIRL TALK books?

Bookstore_____Toy store_____Discount store_____

Grocery store_____Supermarket_____Other (give name)_____

9) Which type of store would you visit most often if you wanted to buy a GIRL TALK book?

Check *only* one: Bookstore_____Toy store_____

Discount store_____Grocery store_____Supermarket_____

Other (give name)_____

10) How many books do you read in a month?

Check one: 0____   1 to 2____   3 to 4 ____   5 or more____

11) Do you read any of these books?

Check those you have read:

The Baby-sitters Club_____   Nancy Drew_____

Pen Pals_____   Sweet Valley High _____

Sweet Valley Twins_____Gymnasts_____

12) Where do you shop most often to buy these books?

Check one: Bookstore_____Toy store_____

Discount store_____Grocery store_____Supermarket_____

Other (give name)_____

13) What other kinds of books do you read most often?

_____

14) What would you like to read more about in GIRL TALK?

_____

_____

Send completed form to :
GIRL TALK Survey Western Publishing Company, Inc.
1220 Mound Avenue, Mail Station #85
Racine, Wisconsin 53404

**LOOK FOR THE AWESOME GIRL TALK BOOKS IN
A STORE NEAR YOU!**

MORE GIRL TALK TITLES TO LOOK FOR

Nonfiction
ASK ALLIE 101 answers to your questions about boys, friends, family, and school!

YOUR PERSONALITY QUIZ Fun, easy quizzes to help you discover the real you!

BOYTALK: HOW TO TALK TO YOUR FAVORITE GUY